Wanted: No Strings

Brandy Ayers

ISBN: **1981513337**
ISBN-13: **978-1981513338**

DEDICATION

To the real Meg, my sister and friend.
I forgive you for dropping me on my head
And trying to kill me as a baby.

CONTENTS

Personal Ad   7

Chapter One   9

Chapter Two   15

Chapter Three   21

Chapter Four   26

Chapter Five   32

Chapter Six   38

Chapter Seven   48

Chapter Eight   58

Chapter Nine   68

Chapter Ten   75

Chapter Eleven   82

Chapter Twelve   90

Chapter Thirteen   96

Epilogue One   105

Epilogue Two   111

About the Author   119

PERSONAL AD
WANTED: BIG DICK, NO STRINGS

I am seeking some no-strings fun with a well-endowed man. I know, I know. Women say this all the time, but they don't really mean it . . . I do.

Recently divorced from a small-dicked asshole who never took any interest in whether or not I came, I have no desire to jump into another relationship anytime soon.

However, I do have lots of other desires. I've only ever slept with one man, in one position, and I've never had an orgasm that didn't involve my own hand.

Now that I'm a free agent, I want to find out what all the fuss is about.

But I have things I need in whoever I decide to play with.

#1 A big dick. Maybe it is shallow, but after spending eight years with a man who I had to ask whether it was in yet, I want to be with a guy who leaves no doubt when he's inside me.

#2 A sense of humor. If we're going to do this, you gotta not be an asshole, and I have to like your personality, at least a little bit.

#3 No cheaters. If you are married or seriously involved, get the eff out of here and pay attention to your woman.

That is about it. I'll want to meet first and sit down for coffee to make sure we get along and you aren't a complete psycho.

And just so you know and won't be disappointed, I am what I like to call curvy and others might call chubby. I have huge tits, hips, and ass. If that isn't your thing, no problem.

Dick pics encouraged.

CHAPTER ONE
Trent

I read the ad again.

And again.

My dick jumps each time.

It is like something out of the porn I watched as a teen on skinamax: The desperate, unsatisfied wife eyeing the pool boy with interest. He showed her all the ways her husband couldn't pleasure her. Only I am a man, and she doesn't have a husband anymore.

"This chick has to be crazy." Brant roars out a laugh that, no lie, shakes the walls. "Does she even know what she's asking for when she says dick pics are encouraged? Idiot is going to get inundated with them."

The guys and I were all sitting around on a lunch break when someone brought up a craigslist ad we absolutely had to read. The five idiots I call employees are all sitting around in hysterics at the ad. But I'm intrigued.

Most the personals ads on craigslist have innocuous titles: looking for the one, looking for a hookup, looking for a friend, looking for a generous friend. But not this one. She laid it all out there right from the get-go. She's looking for a big dick.

I certainly fulfill that requirement. Hell, if she had really been dealing with that little for the past eight years, she might be scared of what I'm packing. Luckily, getting women ready to take all of my monster cock is one of my favorite pastimes.

There is something about the ad and the woman who wrote it that is calling to me. Her sense of humor is obvious. But maybe it is really just my own ego rearing its ugly head. I like the idea of being the one to show this long-suffering, dissatisfied woman how a man should really show his partner pleasure.

Glancing over to make sure the guys are still goofing off, I click Reply on my phone.

Brant is right, though. I'm sure the poor lady had no idea what she was getting herself into when she typed the words "dick pics encouraged." If she'd been out of the game for almost a decade, she might not know how many assholes out there love nothing more than sending women shots of their junk.

So, I'm taking a different tack.

Subject: No dick pic . . . yet

Hey there, saw your ad on craigslist, and I'm intrigued. I'm sure you're getting flooded with dick pics of all shapes and sizes, most probably not pretty. So, I thought I'd give your eyes a break and send you a picture of a kitten instead. There, don't you feel better? Now that I have cleansed your palate, I'd very much like to grab coffee with you sometime so we can get to know each other, then see where things go from there. I've included a picture of myself, with pants on. If you're still interested, email back.

PS The more curves the better in my book.

I attach the photo one of my sisters took of me chopping wood at our parents' cabin, and send it to my mystery lady.

"Okay, assholes, this house isn't going to restore itself. Back to work." I ball up the rest of my trash and throw it in the nearest barrel. This is going to be one long, hard day full of manual labor. But I wouldn't have it any other way.

It will keep my mind off the mystery woman and her ad. And whether she'll take me up on my offer for coffee. Damn, I hope she does.

The guys and I spread out through the second floor of the house, or what is left of it. About two weeks ago, a space heater tipped over in one of the rooms and set the whole place on fire. From what I understand, the family that lived here had fallen on hard times, and they were all sleeping in one room heated by the one space heater. Thank God, the mom smelled the smoke and got them all out in time. She had some minor burns but managed to save her two kids, husband, and even the family cat.

Of course, in an effort to save more money, they had let their homeowner's insurance lapse, which is where I came in. If anyone saw me right now, they would think I was just some blue-collar schmuck doing backbreaking work for pennies on the dollar.

They'd be fucking wrong.

And that is why I hate snobs and anyone who makes a snap judgement based off appearances. The truth is, I have a net worth just south of Bill Gates. I've designed some of the most reliable and sophisticated software that helps law enforcement, 911 call centers, and fire stations do their jobs more precisely. I sold that to damn near every city, county, state, and government office in the country. Gave it away to just as many. That, in addition to the twenty-plus other apps and tech innovations I've sold over the years, and I can do pretty much anything I want to these days. Including start up a nonprofit that rehabilitates homes damaged due to fires, floods, and other circumstances beyond the owner's control, houses that would otherwise sit and become an eyesore in the community. Despite my nerd origins, I've always loved getting dirty and sweaty.

Hopefully, I'll be getting dirty and sweaty with a repressed woman very soon.

Despite my best intentions, the ad and my response are

never far from my mind. I've never been this hung up about a woman in all my life, and I know nothing about her other than her ex was an idiot. Any man who makes his woman's pleasure come a distant second to his own has to be an idiot. As far as I'm concerned, I should come once for every three orgasms I give a woman. By the end of a night in my bed, women are exhausted, but satisfied.

Come to think of it, it's been a while since anyone graced my bed other than my dog Honey Badger.

"Yo, boss, you gonna keep busting up that wall until it's dust, or is that good enough?" Fuck. Brant could be a loudmouthed idiot, but he had a point.

The studs I had been knocking down were indeed pulverized to mere splinters, slightly overzealous on my part. "Yeah, yeah. How about you focus on your work and stop critiquing my technique, asshole."

Brant put down his sledgehammer and ambled over my way, grabbing a water bottle out of the cooler on the way. "You were awfully quiet during lunch. What's the deal?"

Loudmouthed asshole or not, he is also my best friend. My best friend who apparently doesn't miss a goddamned thing.

"No deal. Just didn't feel like acting like a couple of girls giggling over dirty words in a romance novel." Carefully avoiding his eyes, I get back to work on the next section of wall. We had already demoed the attic and roof. The second floor was this week and would be completely leveled. Thankfully, the first floor was in pretty good shape. We would just need to replace the Sheetrock, flooring, appliances, and furniture. But at least it wasn't a complete loss. It gave the homeowners a little bit of solace when they knew we had been able to save at least a little bit of their original home, even if it was only the studs.

"Man, you think I'm some sort of dumbass, huh, Trent?" Trailing behind me, the guy just will not let up. "Seriously, dude. Something about that ad we were reading pique your interest? I know how you love to be the superman of orgasms. You think about answering the lady?"

"Pretty sure he already did," Hardy shouts from the other side of the house.

This, right here, is the problem with working with your five best friends. Nothing freaking slips by them.

"Fuck it." I sling my hammer over my shoulder and face the men who have been by my side since we met in college and designed the first dating website targeted specifically at college students. "Yes, I answered her ad. Just because I'm not the marrying kind doesn't mean I can't give some poor former housewife a ride on the tripod."

"I knew it!" Razor comes out of nowhere and circles the group with an outstretched hand, the rest of the guys all whipping out their wallets and slapping twenty-dollar bills into his palm. "Pay up, motherfuckers."

"What the hell?" These guys are getting on my last nerve today.

"As soon as I read that ad I knew you'd be all over it like glitter on a stripper," Razor, so named for his preferred mode of transportation back when we were poor college students, says. "I said you'd answer the ad before lunch was over. Brant said you'd wait until we got back to work and you could be alone. Hardy called 'waiting until you got home.' Smith had 'not answering at all.' Smith always was a shit gambler."

"Fuck you, Razor." Smith's voice echoes out from the now cavernous bathroom.

Despite these guys being a pain in my ass, I have to laugh. They know me better than anyone ever has. "Alright, numbskulls. Back to work. Drinks are apparently on Razor tonight."

The guys turn back to their tasks, as do I. But despite focusing on the work at hand, I can't deny that a little part of my brain stays focused on whether I would have an email waiting for me at the end of the day.

CHAPTER TWO
Francie

"Holy shit, Fran. Check this one out!" Meg yells from the other room, her voice filled with barely contained laughter.

I stopped looking at the pictures about two hours ago. Two hours after I woke up from a night of celebrating my new single status. Two hours after I discovered in my drunken state I had posted a very ill-advised personal ad on craigslist.

An ad asking for dick pics.

I will never live this one down.

"No thanks. You seen one dick, you've seen them all, I have discovered." Damn if that wasn't the truth. I honestly don't know why I thought this was a good idea last night. The two bottles of wine I downed probably had a lot to do with it.

"No, seriously, this one is pierced." Meg sounded hypnotized. Okay, maybe I would check this one out. "In fact, can I answer this guy? I think that might be fun."

I pad over to her spot on the couch where my laptop sits on her knees and lean over to check out the latest in a long line of penis-mail. It is a cell picture close-up of a guy's junk, and indeed there is a barbell sticking out not only through the head of the guy's dick, but another in the middle and one at the base.

"Wow, that is kind of scary. But intriguing. I think my first time out should not be with a guy who has more jewelry in his crotch than I wear on my entire body." Despite the ad probably being a bad idea, I've decided I'm going through with it. I want to have random sex with a well-hung stranger. Call me weird. Call me a slut. I don't give a shit. I deserve this after spending eight years with a borderline emotionally abusive asshole of a husband who wouldn't know his way to an erogenous zone if he had GPS turn-by-turn directions.

Standing back up, I head to the kitchen to clean up the mess we made last night. Apparently, we thought s'mores would pair well with red wine, but thought messing with fire while drinking would be a bad idea. So, we used the microwave instead. Now the entire inside of the damn thing is coated in the results of leaving a marshmallow in for a full two minutes.

"Wait, FranFran. Come back. I found a winner." Meg is practically bouncing in her seat in excitement. I don't trust that reaction one bit. It is the same exact reaction she gave to the guy who sent me a picture of his dick dressed up like Abraham Lincoln. Top hat included.

"Yeah right, Meg. I'm not falling for that again." The scent of lemon and bleach hits me as soon as I cross back into my tiny kitchen in my brand-new apartment. I don't care whether it is the size of my former house's laundry room, I freaking love this apartment. Because it is mine. The only name on the lease is Francie Lee. Not Francie Hudson. Francie Hudson was a doormat stuck in a big house with a petty little man who had somehow tricked her into marrying him at eighteen, before she had ever seen the world.

Practically skipping into the kitchen, Meg held out the laptop for me to see. "I'm serious, Fran. This is the guy. He sent a picture of a kitten and a picture of himself shirtless chopping wood. But real wood. Not dick wood."

Holy. Shit.

This guy is beyond gorgeous. I can't tell how tall he is from the photo, but I'm guessing around six foot, judging by the way his long arms dwarf the ax in his hands by comparison. His tan skin is glistening with sweat, dark hair is covered on top by a Steelers cap, and jeans are riding low on his hips. The photo was taken at the perfect moment so it got the ax as he swung it high over his head, before bringing it down on the log in front of him. I had no idea arms had that many muscles in them.

"No, no way. That guy is way too hot for me. Let's aim a little lower, sis." Don't misunderstand, I think I'm attractive. It took a while for me to get to this place where I accept my body and appreciate it for its curves. Years of my ex telling me I needed to lose thirty pounds were hard to overcome. But the past year and lots of hard work brought me a long way.

Still, this guy is out of JLaw's league. He is next-level hot. We're talking put-him-on-a-billboard-in-Times-Square hot.

I see myself going more for a Chris Pratt pre-*Zero Dark Thirty*. *Parks and Rec* Chris Pratt, that's more my comfort zone.

"Fran, so help me, if you do not email this guy back, I will call you at three in the morning as I am rolling home from shift every night until you do." Meg props one hand on her hip, the other still holding my laptop, and gives me her best sass face. "Besides, he said right here, 'The more curves the better in my book.' See, he likes a little junk in the trunk. Go for it!"

I whine a little, not wanting to go quite that far out on a limb. Posting the ad and then not deleting it once I sobered up is enough of a character break. But pursuing a blazing hot guy like this? No way.

Still, if there is one thing Meg takes seriously, it is her threats. She once told me if I didn't apply to college, she would stop coloring my hair for me. That was nine years ago. I let my ex talk me into working while he did college, and my highlights haven't been the same since.

"Okay, I'll answer his email, but I'm attaching a picture too so he can bow out if he wants. I really don't want to go through the whole he-sees-me-at-the-coffee-shop-and-decides-to-bail nightmare scenario." Rereading his email makes me smirk a little. He was right on about needing a break from dick pics. My inbox is teeming with dicks of all sizes. "What should I say? I suck at this."

"You're just rusty. Once you get your sea legs back, this whole thing will be easy like Sunday morning." Meg pulls the laptop out from under my frozen fingers. "Here we go. 'Thanks for the reply and for not sending a dick pic. A little too much wine may have gone into that line.'"

"Good. Now say, 'The kitten was a perfect break for my bleeding eyes.'" Okay, this is actually kind of fun.

"Yes! 'Maybe if things work out, you can get an up close and personal look at my pussycat.'" Meg giggles like crazy, nearly dropping my very expensive and very necessary-for-work laptop on the floor.

"You cannot say that. That is so cheesy and not me." I slide the computer back over to me and delete that last line. "'I also very much enjoyed the picture of you chopping wood. I figure I should return the favor by enclosing a picture of myself. This is from a photo shoot my sister made me do after I filed for divorce.'"

"Shut up! Are you really going to send him one of the boudoir photos?" Meg bounces on the balls of her feet, the excitement coursing through her needing some sort of outlet.

"Might as well show him the goods. If he's still into it after seeing my thunder thighs, then I'll give it a shot too." I pick my favorite of the photos. In it I'm wearing a big cream sweater that covers my tummy, but the oversized cowl-neck is slung low on my shoulder, with one breast almost entirely exposed. The hem of the sweater ends just at my hips, and my hands grip the center of it, as if I'm trying to pull it down to cover my pussy. There is just a hint of the red panties I had been wearing, that's it. My legs are bare, crossed at the ankles, and I'm up on my tippy-toes. One lip caught between my teeth and the blowout to end all blowouts finish off the innocent yet sultry look.

Truth is I am incredibly thankful Meg made me do these photos with a friend of hers. I felt sexy while doing them, and every time I see them I recall that feeling. Derek, my ex, still insists on leaving berating voicemail messages a couple times a week, despite being separated for a year. I have a sneaking suspicion the fact our divorce is now final won't make a damn bit of difference, and he'll continue with the messages telling me how useless I have always been. But when he calls, I just look at these photos and remind myself that I am a sexy bitch, and I'm better without his lazy ass.

"Okay, how about this for a closing? 'If you like what you see, and still want to get coffee, let me know.'"

"Can you at least put something like, 'I can't wait to let my kitty climb all over your wood?'"

That spark of humor I love so much ignites in my sister's eyes. And just to make her happy, I include her stupid line. I don't tell her that I add a postscript that my sister made me say it. "Okay, here goes nothing."

Clicking Send on that email feels like a huge accomplishment. An even bigger achievement than starting my business last year and making it grow. This is the first step to exploring my sexuality and sensuality. I didn't lie in that ad. I really don't want a relationship right now. I want to let loose, experiment.

I met Derek my sophomore year in high school. He was a junior, a basketball player, and so sweet in the beginning. He was patient when I didn't want to have sex yet, then stayed close to go to college. As soon as I turned eighteen, he proposed. My parents were furious, but I accepted, and we had a small justice of the peace ceremony. That night we had painful, underwhelming sex for the first time. The first of many. The changes were subtle, but consistent. He became more controlling, shorter, more terse. Then somehow over the years, I found myself being a near hermit, living with a man I no longer knew, who made me feel like shit on a daily basis. The last straw had been when he openly compared me to other women we knew and always found me lacking.

But all that is behind me now. Regardless of whether this man would want to kick off my age of awakening, I am starting down the road to figuring out what I want in and out of bed. At twenty-six, it is about damn time.

CHAPTER THREE
Trent

I have never been this nervous in all my life. Despite the soothing decor this cafe has going on, my heart is racing a mile a minute, my leg won't stop bouncing, and I've been sporting a halfie since opening Fran's reply to me three days ago.

That picture. Fuck, that picture. I've jacked off to the picture of her in that big sweater countless times in the last seventy-two hours. I haven't masturbated this much since I was a teenager and discovered my parents got all the movie channels on cable and late at night they showed soft-core porn. The crazy thing is everything of interest had been covered in the picture. But I could picture it all hiding under there. Huge melon tits, soft belly, wide hips, and the sweetest pussy a man could dream of, all hidden under a bulky sweater. And that peek of red lace at her hip. Fuck, I almost died right there.

We've emailed back and forth a couple times since that first day, and everything I've learned about Fran points to her being a cool-ass chick, with a dirty fucking mind. Because we've gone there through emails. I asked her what her dirtiest fantasy was, but on no planet did I ever think she would say multiple men pleasuring her at once. She assured me it was only something she liked to think about, and not something she was actually interested in doing. Which is good, because I wasn't really into the whole sharing thing. But I could definitely think of some ways to give her a similar thrill.

The coffee in this place is pretty damn spectacular but doing nothing to soothe my nerves. I'll have to ask Fran how she found this place. It's a little hole-in-the-wall coffee shop slash bar, but without the creepy meat market vibe of a normal bar. More like a coffee place that happens to also serve whiskey. My large frame must look comical on the overstuffed velvet love seat I chose to sit in. I debated getting a table but didn't want anything between us to keep me from touching her.

A cool burst of air swirls inside the dining room as the door opens. There she is, finally. She isn't late, but I was ridiculously early. Her eyes scan the perimeter of the space, and I stand so she can see me past the swarm of weekend patrons.

As soon as our gazes connect, her whole face lights up. Fuck. No one has ever smiled like that for me before. Part excitement, part shyness, part innocence. My dick grows even more, and I thank the denim gods for keeping it contained.

Francie weaves through the tables and people, taking what feels like an eternity to reach me. When she does, I can't help myself. I need to feel her skin. In a fog, I lean in and brush my lips against her cheek, my hands gripping her hips. The need to take it further, capture her lips between mine, throw her on the velvet couch behind me, and feast on her is nearly overwhelming.

Her skin is just as soft as I imagined. My lips linger on her round cheek for a moment more than is probably appropriate, and I'm rewarded with a little hitch in her breath and her body rocking slightly closer to mine.

"Nice to meet you, Francie." I lean back and take in her stunned expression. Her cheeks are bright red and her eyes dilated.

Fuck. I told myself I wouldn't try to sleep with her tonight. This is just supposed to be an initial meet and greet, with the possibility of fucking at our next get-together. I get it. She needs to ease into this, and I'm willing to jump through any damn hoops she wants to put in my way.

But the way she's looking at me right now is making it very hard to live up to that agreement. Fire lives in those green eyes. Just looking at her, I immediately know her ex wasted his time with Francie. There is a wildcat inside her just waiting to be unleashed. And I plan to be the one setting it free.

Her long dark hair hangs in loose waves around her face. Visions of gathering it into a ponytail in my hand as she sucks me deep into her throat fill my filthy mind. The dress covering all those sinful curves is modest in a way. Everything is covered, barely even a hint of cleavage. But the thing hugs her body in a way that has me ready to sit up and beg for any scrap of attention she's willing to throw my way. It stops just above her knees, and her smooth calves curve down to heels that I immediately know I'll be asking her to wear again and not take them off as I drive into her sweet pussy.

Finished with my slow perusal of her body, I take a deep breath, willing my damn body to cooperate. Fucking finally, I find my voice, but none of the smooth things I'd been practicing before she arrived come out. "Fuck, you're gorgeous."

Her blush deepens, and I imagine her cheeks are currently the same color as her nipples, which are poking out in a silent salute beneath her dress.

"Thank you." Unable to meet my heated gaze, she shifts her focus to her shoes, which just won't do. I want her looking at me.

Hooking my finger under her chin, I guide her face up, locking her eyes with my own. "I want those emerald greens on me, baby. Never look down when we're together."

The side of her lush lips quirks up into an amused grin. "So, you're not into subservient women then?"

"Oh, I have no problems with a little role-playing, but mostly I like a woman who knows she gives me an instant hard-on, even fully clothed." Taking another step closer, I brush my lips across her ear and press my rigid length against her soft belly. "And I've been hard since I first laid eyes on that picture."

Francie is even more wild than I originally thought, because she shocks the shit out of me by snaking her delicate little hand between us to stroke my length beneath my jeans.

"Well, I guess this answers the question of whether or not you meet my size requirement, since you refused to send me a dick pic." The slight pout of her bottom lip makes me want to bite it, and I just barely hold myself back.

"If you don't cut that out, I'm not going to be able to make good on my promise not to fuck you tonight." Goddamn, her hand just keeps going. We're surrounded by people, and it has to look at least a little weird that we've been standing so close, almost in a hug, and whispering in each other's ears.

"You don't want to fuck me tonight?" Her pout is clear as day in her voice, which I can't see because I have to close my eyes to keep from coming in my pants. "But I've been all wet and needy for you since all those sexy things you said in your emails. I thought about not wearing panties tonight, but I was afraid you would make my juices run down my thigh just from sitting next to you."

Holy shit. I think I've met my match. No woman has ever thrown me off my game like this. I always have complete control over my desires. Not tonight though.

"We need to leave." I'm panting in her ear, the soft strands of her hair dancing from the force of my breaths.

Her hand drops away from my crotch, and she steps back. I follow. I never again want there to be that much distance between our bodies.

"Did you change your mind? Am I being too forward?" The fire and lust in her eyes quickly gets replaced by unmistakable fear.

I shake my head firmly, wanting there to be absolutely no fucking doubts in her head. "Oh no, this is happening. But I don't want the first time I hear you screaming my name to be in the middle of a coffee shop while people sip their drinks and watch me pound into your pussy."

Her breath comes out in little huffs of arousal. Thank God for craigslist, because I can't believe I might have missed out on this girl had my friends not seen her ad. "You like that thought, don't you? You like the idea of all these people watching how undone you make me. How I'll punish you with my hands against your ass while my cock is shoved deep inside you?"

She nods slightly, obviously embarrassed by her little kink for exhibition.

"We'll play with that another time. Right now I need to get you behind closed doors so I can do whatever I want to you. Understand?"

"Yes, please."

"Good girl. Remember those two little words. You'll be saying them a lot in my presence."

CHAPTER FOUR
Francie

Holy shit.

I can't believe this is happening. I am actually doing this. I'm going to hook up with a complete stranger. Okay, not complete stranger. We've talked over email and Google Chat a few times. But still.

I can't believe the first time I have sex with someone other than my asshole ex-husband is going to be with a stranger.

Everything about Trent is big. He's tall. Broad. And the bulge in his pants is more than a little intimidating. But apart from the physical aspects, he also has presence. He drew my eye immediately when I walked in, and I'm not the only one. People around us notice him. Women and men.

Trent grabs my hand and practically drags me to the door of the cafe, urgency screaming from every tense muscle in his body. We burst out onto the icy sidewalk, and I almost bite it in the ridiculous heels my sister talked me into wearing. Thankfully, a thick arm wraps around my waist, steadying me against his side.

"Your place or mine?" White puffs of breath circle us as Trent pants beside me.

It takes a minute for the question to penetrate. My place or his? Shit. I don't know. If we go to his place, God knows what I'm walking into. He could have a dungeon beneath the floorboards of his living room where he keeps all the unsuspecting girls he picks up off craigslist.

So, my place.

But is that any better? He is a stranger. Do I really want to let this guy who I barely know in on where I spend ninety-five percent of my time? He could be a crazy stalker that waits in my hall every day for a glimpse of me.

So, not my place.

A hotel? Is that too seedy? It seems a little prostitute-ish to take a dude I just met to a hotel so we can bang.

"Stop thinking, Francie." Trent spins me into his chest, covering my mouth with his and chasing every bit of hesitation away. "Where to?"

"My place. It's close." I turn, and this time it is me dragging him down the street. For a moment I'm a little embarrassed that he is going to see what I've been calling my rebound apartment. I went from having a fabulous historic brick mini-mansion in the North Hills to a shoebox-sized studio apartment on the South Side. I had no desire to take any of the asshat's money, so I'm living on my income alone now. I'm learning to budget and save and pay bills for the first time, since Derek had me on an allowance and never let me have access to our bank accounts.

Remembering that fact goes a long way to erasing my concerns about what Trent will think of my place. Who gives a flying shit what he thinks? I'm on my own now. Everything I have is mine and mine alone. I'm proud of my place and what I've done with it. If he doesn't like it, well then, he doesn't have to fuck me tonight.

"This is me." I pull my keys from my purse and unlock the stairwell door. We barely make it in the door before Trent has my front pinned against the cold brick wall. His warm mouth sucks and nibbles on my neck and shoulder, the clashing of cold and hot sending goose bumps along my skin.

"Thank fuck." The words caress my skin as he sighs the words against me. "Another block and I was going to pull you into an alley just to get a taste of your pussy."

Fuck. That's hot. I want that.

I had no idea the thought of doing it in public would turn me on so much. But then, I have no idea about anything when it comes to me and sex. It is past time I start learning though.

One of Trent's hands slides down my side, tracing the curves I'm only just starting to appreciate. He gathers the hem of my dress in his palm and drags it up my thigh until my hip and half my ass are exposed to him. Slowly, so slowly I think I might have an orgasm simply from the intense anticipation seeping through my body, his fingers trace back down to between my legs.

"No panties." The statement comes out part reverence, part curse. "You're a bad girl, Francie." His hand disappears momentarily before the sharp sting of his palm on my skin singes my ass. "I like that about you."

He bites the space where my neck meets my shoulders and backs away enough for me to lead him through the dark alley that connects to the equally dark stairs. I walk with the skirt still rucked up around my waist, my bare ass hanging out for him to see. I wonder briefly whether he can see my arousal dripping down my inner thighs.

We both practically sprint up the stairs, almost crashing into the wall at the top of the landing. Then we're stumbling past my joke of a kitchen, Trent's hands exploring my body as we go. He presses me against the wall beside my bed, which I normally leave folded up into the wall, but left down and actually made just for this occasion.

Before I can react, the zipper on my dress is undone, and he shoves the whole thing to the ground. I'm standing with my palms pressed to the smooth drywall in nothing but a bra and heels.

I've never felt more alive in my entire life.

"Jesus, what perfume do you wear?" Trent runs his nose down my spine until he's kneeling behind me. "Smells so good I want to drown in it."

"No perfume." I barely get the words out thanks to the hormones swamping my body and dulling my senses. "I use coconut oil for everything. I always smell a little like it."

Trent groans behind me while he licks the small dimples above my ass. His hands seem to be everywhere. Running up and down my legs. Thank God I waxed. Over my hips. Don't think about the weight I carry there. Deft fingers grip the five hooks and eyes on my bra, needed to keep the girls up and at attention, and flicks it open. I let the bra fall to the ground and nearly lose my mind when his hands cup my breasts, lifting them as if taking their measure.

"These tits are fucking insane. Turn around." That demanding voice sends shivers from my head to toes, and I'm helpless to resist.

Midturn it dawns on me that the lights are still on in here. Like, every single light. It is one of my many weird quirks that have developed now that I live alone. I don't like coming home to an empty apartment. The alley and stairs are bad enough. So, every single light in my little place is blazing from the time I wake up to the time I go to sleep. Something I am wholeheartedly regretting now that the world's most impossibly hot man is kneeling before me, nothing hiding the rolls, cellulite, and saggy boobs that have haunted me since puberty. My hands twitch with the need to cover myself up. A man hasn't seen me in my birthday suit since my ex saw me get out of the shower two years before I left him. He made a comment about needing to cut back on the cheese because it was all collecting in my thighs.

My body and brain are at war with conflicting ideas.

Brain: hurry and turn the lights off, apologize to this poor man for subjecting his beautiful eyes to your pale, frumpy body, and show him to the door.

Body: Fuck. That. No. Fuck. Him.

I clasp my hands in front of my freshly waxed pussy, weaving my fingers together over and over. My skin prickles as his eyes travel across every naked inch of me, and I avoid looking at his face at all costs.

But he'll have none of that apparently. Trent grips my chin and guides my gaze back to his, just as he did back at the coffee shop. "You are the most stunningly beautiful woman I've ever had the privilege to touch."

Tears burn behind my eyes. Don't cry. Don't fucking do it. You cannot cry when the hot one-night stand you picked up off craigslist says the nicest thing anyone has ever said to you. "You don't have to say that. I'm a sure thing. No need to work all that hard for it."

Anger flashes in his eyes for a fraction of a second before it relaxes into the heated, sexy stare he's been giving me all night. "I don't say things I don't mean." Trent effortlessly climbs to his feet and takes a step back. "Get on the bed, face up."

Bed. Yes. I can do this. I try to find my way back to the sexy temptress I had channeled back in the coffee shop, but she seems to have left the building along with my clothes. Still, I don't want this to end, so I'll fake it.

Sitting on the edge of the bed, I scoot back until I'm right smack in the middle of the lumpy mattress. As I ease down into a reclining position, I can't figure out how to best arrange my limbs so they don't flatten out unattractively on the bed.

All thoughts go the way of the dodo bird at the first brush of Trent's lips against my ankles.

"I've jerked off more times than I can count to thoughts of your slender ankles locked behind my back as I drill into your tight pussy." He licks up to the curve of my calf on one leg, then back down on the other. "I've pictured gripping these curvy legs and pushing them out as far as they will go to give me better access." Rough fingers graze up my inner thighs, swooping around to palm my hips. "Dreamt about leaving bruises so deep you can see my fingerprints on your pale skin from holding you while you ride me, pushing your sweet body down onto my cock."

He keeps going, avoiding all the super interesting areas, the areas weeping for his touch, and I suddenly want to cry again. No one has ever worshipped my body like this. Ever made me feel as sexy as this near stranger has in less time than I could imagine. The temptress is on her way back. Not even his hand grazing across my slightly rounded tummy can deny her appearance. Because Trent wants me. This man who could have anyone thinks my body is sexy. I know this not only because of the sweet, hot words tumbling from his mouth in rough whispers but because his rock-hard dick his currently digging into my leg through his pants. I made him that hard. I've barely touched him, and he is already harder than I ever thought possible.

CHAPTER FIVE
Trent

Whoever tore down this amazing woman beneath me deserves to be pounded into the ground. I have the baffling need to get Francie off as many times as is humanly possible, show her what her gorgeous body can do, then go find her dipshit of an ex and teach him how to treat women. All women. Regardless of size, shape, color, or any other defining characteristic.

I'm a big believer that all women are things of beauty in some way. It may not always be obvious on the outside, but dig a little deeper and you'll find that spark that makes them sexy and irresistible.

The thing that pisses me off the most is you don't have to look for what makes Francie beautiful. It is right there in front of me. Quivering as my fingers trace the bottom curves of her breasts. In the blazing heat of her eyes. The wicked, kinky temptress who I know lives inside her, waiting to be coaxed out. I'm going to be the one to open her up, watch her blossom.

Then I'm going to be the one to claim her as mine and mine alone.

Somewhere between emailing back and forth and crawling into this bed, I've decided this is no one-night stand. She doesn't know it yet, but in addition to being her kinky-sex tour guide, I'm also going to be the one she grows old with. Even if I have to use multiple orgasms to convince her of that fact.

"These tits." My cock throbs inside my pants, begging to be released and let him take control. But I have to hold him back. Have to show this woman she is worth so much more than a fast and furious fuck. "There are so many things I want to do with these puppies." Cupping them in my hands, I push her generous breasts together. There is no way I could hold them in my palms without the silky mounds overflowing. They're big, really big. And I won't deny I'm a little obsessed with them. By the increase in Francie's breathing, I can tell she likes having her tits played with. That will work out well for me.

"What would you do with them? To them." The words are barely audible through her shallow panting.

"Lick them until they're glistening, then blow on them until they pucker so tight you beg me to soothe them with my tongue again." Gently, giving just a hint of what I'm describing, I swirl the tip of my tongue around one dusty rose nipple. Backing off, I push them even closer together. "I'd make you hold them together just like this while I fuck my cock in and out of the tight valley between. I'd pinch your nipples so hard you'd be writhing right on the edge of pain and pleasure. Then I'd release them, allow the blood to rush back into your aching tips, and hold your mouth open as I come on your tongue, spilling my seed all over your chest and neck as I go. I'd make you messy. I'd mark you."

Francie is practically dancing beneath me, her body unable to stay still with the desire pulsing through it. I can see it in her eyes. The need for me to follow through on my fantasies. The need to explode in a riot of sensations. But I'm not going to do any of that to her today. Because what I've described is all about me taking my pleasure from her body. Tonight is all about giving her body as much pleasure as is humanly possible. For that, I need to put my own desires aside. But really, I'm not. Because fulfilling her needs is the base motive for everything I do from this moment forward.

I grip her hands and bring them up to the wall, pressing her palms against the faded paint. "Don't move. If I see your palms move so much as an inch, I'll be forced to punish you."

"Fuck, why does that sound good?" She's practically whining.

"Because you're a dirty girl. Just the way I like it." I slither down between her thighs, licking and sucking as I go. Francie keeps trying to say something, but words fail her each time I move to worship another part of her body. Finally, I settle with my face front and center before her beautiful pussy. Her swollen lips are bare, except for a small patch just above her slit. "I like this." I toy with her soft curls, tugging them, then running my fingers over them slightly.

"The . . . the waxer was mad I insisted on leaving a little something. I-I didn't like the idea of being totally bare." She stumbles over her words, obviously struggling to get them out through her mounting pleasure.

"Good choice." I lick a straight line down her slit, not hard enough to part her lips and graze her clit, but enough to make her hiss and suck her breath in.

"Trent, um, you really don't need to spend a whole lot of time down there. I've never been able to come from, um, you know, uh, that."

Jesus, her shy hesitance is fucking turning me on. And somehow, I'm happy beyond measure that I'll be the first person to give her an orgasm using my mouth alone. "You mean no one has ever eaten your pussy until you screamed so loud the walls shook?"

"Oh God, not even close." Gazing up her body, I see her eyes are screwed shut so tight little wrinkles are popping up all over her forehead.

"Francie, open your eyes. Look at me." Like a good girl, she does as I ask, and the uncertainty there just won't do right now. If this is going to work, she needs to be right here with me. "Make no mistake, my dirty girl, there is no place else I want to be right now than with my whole face buried in your pussy." I keep my eye contact with her and part those puffy lower lips with my thumbs, spreading her open for me. On instinct, her knees fall open just a little more, and that makes me grin. Her body knows what it wants. "I'm not going to mention the idiot who wasted his time with you again after this, but his failings have nothing to do with you. I'm about to show you what this body can do. That you can come so many times in one night you lose count and forget your own name. Starting here." I slick my tongue over every fold, around her entrance, then once right on her clit. The room echoes with her desperate moans and whimpers. She's so close, and I've barely done anything. "You're going to watch me as I eat this pussy up and drink down all your juices. The first time will be only with my tongue and lips. The second time I'll add in fingers. The third, fourth, and fifth will be on my cock. Got it?"

She clamps her teeth down on her bottom lip and nods eagerly. Now she's with me.

I don't waste any time. I need to taste her, deep in her pussy where my cock will soon be. I shove my tongue into her tight walls, and her hips shoot off the bed in surprise pleasure. But she keeps her hands planted right where I left them, just as I told her to. Francie's essence explodes across my taste buds. Sweet, a little salty, and the most addicting thing I've ever had in my mouth. I crave more, and the only way to get it is to have her coming so hard it is pouring out of her.

Reluctantly, I draw out of her, pressing against her front wall as I go. Experimenting a little, I start to figure out exactly what she likes. I suck her folds into my mouth, circle her clit with my tongue, and dip it back into her eager hole. It all makes her shake and pant like a woman crazed. But what makes her let go and explode is when I nibble on her clit, then suck it hard and fast into my mouth, flicking my tongue over it at the same time. The orgasm hits her hard and fast. I haven't even been between her legs for more than five minutes when it happens.

She's a live wire, squirming as if she wants to get away from me one second, then thrusting her pussy into my face the next. Words fall from her mouth in torrents, none of them connecting to make a coherent thought. "Fuck . . . Damn . . . Don't stop." Not to mention damn near every deity known to man is praised at some point. Through it all her eyes never leave mine, our connection so intense I can feel it leaving an imprint on my soul.

The very second she starts to come down from her climax, I thrust two fingers into her tight pussy, and she's off again. Searching with my fingertips, I find the patch of bumpy flesh that every man should know by heart, but far too many ignore. I work it as if my life depends on it, brushing it in light circles, then pressing on it in pulsing waves. All the while I suck and nibble her clit.

My efforts are rewarded with a flood of her arousal seeping from between my fingers, coating my mouth and dripping down my chin. Not only did I make her come from oral sex, something she apparently didn't think possible, I made her fucking gush. I won't deny the surge of pride that fills me with that knowledge. I want to sit back on my knees and beat my chest like a caveman. But I resist, instead staying with her through not only her second orgasm of the night but straight into her third.

Once her pussy stops pulsing, I push back, standing at the end of the bed to shed my clothes. The fact that they are all still on hadn't even occurred to me until just now when the need to get my cock inside her became too much to resist. Her eyes follow me, and her hands are still dutifully pressed above her head. Even after all that, she's still following my orders.

As my pants fall to the floor, revealing my hard and angry cock, Francie gasps and her eyes widen.

"How do you walk around with that thing all day? Doesn't it get in the way?" One of her hands flies to cover her mouth. "I can't believe I just said that," she mumbles between her fingers.

I try hard not to laugh, but fail. This woman is too much. Smart and funny. Sexy and yet innocent. "When you've had it your whole life, you get used to it." Moving fast, I kneel beside her on the bed and flip her onto her stomach. "You moved your hand." A sharp crack reverberates through her tiny apartment when I slap her ass. "I told you there would be punishment."

I spank her again, her round cheek pinking up with the imprint of my hand. Fuck, that is hot. I thrust two fingers deep into her pussy, then slap her ass again with my other hand. Her walls contract around me as I dole out too more spanks.

"Looks like someone likes my brand of discipline. Your pussy is practically begging for more."

"I had no idea I would ever like this, but holy shit, I want that big dick inside me while you spank me more." She cranes her neck around, her eyes telling me everything I need to know. "Please."

"As you wish." Gripping her hips, I climb off the bed, pulling her with me so she is kneeling on the floor, bent over the side of the mattress. The damn Murphy bed is so low to the floor I have to kneel too. I line my cock up with her entrance and slam home at the same time my hand smacks across her fleshy ass. It jiggles and shakes with tremors, the movement mesmerizing me for a moment.

My cock throbs inside her tight walls. She spasms and bucks against me, and I have to fight with all my strength not to come inside her right then.

"Oh God, yes, more." This girl, she's my every dirty fantasy come true. And I'm going to give her everything she wants.

CHAPTER SIX
Francie

Holy shit. The things this man is doing to me. The things I'm asking him to do. A few years ago, they wouldn't have even crossed my mind. But now, with his cock shoved so deep inside me I feel an unfamiliar stinging slash stretching that is more pleasure than pain, and his hand slapping my butt, then rubbing away that sting too, it all felt necessary. No wonder I had never been able to come from sex alone before. I'd never been handled this way.

Trent rooted himself to the hilt inside me, his balls pressed against my throbbing, swollen clit. And then stopped, not moving in the slightest. Before I can ask whether something is wrong, he climbs to his feet, both hands gripping my hips and pulling me up with him so I am bent in half at the waist, hands braced on the bed, still filled completely by him. Once we're both firmly standing, he resumes pumping in and out of me in a way that causes my eyes to roll back.

Places inside me I had no idea existed are brushed and pushed with the blunt head of his cock. Each plunge of him into my body inches me closer and closer to an orgasm so intense that it quite frankly scares me a little bit.

Surely it isn't possible to actually pass out from pleasure, right? I know I read about it in a few of the books I edited, but it's just something that women liked to read about: being given so much pleasure at once that your whole world goes black, and all that exists is sensation pouring through every inch of your body. But that can't be real.

Trent's arms snake around me, gripping both my breasts. He toys with my nipples, pulling and twisting them as he continues his brutal pace behind me. I'm teetering on the edge of ecstasy, but find myself holding back. Not wanting to take that plunge and have this all be over.

"Don't do that, sweetheart. Let go. I can feel you resisting it. Trust me. It won't be the last time I make you scream tonight."

God, how did this man read my mind so easily? Or is it just my body he is reading? I decide to trust him. I don't know why. We haven't known each other for more than a few hours. But in this short time, it has become obvious that for tonight at least, his top priority is my pleasure.

So, I give in.

The orgasm explodes through me the moment I let go. I relax at the same time every muscle contracts, overwhelmed with bliss. I know I'm being loud, but none of it penetrates the roar of my first amazing sexual experience. I see stars spread throughout the inky black that overtakes my vision. My fingers curl around handfuls of sheets, yanking and pulling in an effort to ground myself to something, anything.

One minute I'm still hanging bent in half, the next Trent pulls me up so my back is to his chest. One of his huge hands gently cradles my throat, angling my head to the side so he can devour my mouth. The other bands across my stomach, holding me tight as he continues to pump up and into my still pulsing pussy.

"Do you remember how many times I said you would come on my cock?" He speaks around my lips, not bothering to pull back even a centimeter to get the words out. I swallow those rough words, make them part of me now. His voice is shredded. If I didn't know better, I would think it is almost emotional. But that would be ridiculous. This is a one-night stand. One night of amazing fucking, no emotions involved.

Once his question penetrates my lust fog, I think back to what he said before. "Three. You said I would come on your cock three times."

"And that was one. Get ready for two and three."

Before I can respond, Trent pulls out, spins me around, and presses me against the wall. He picks up one of my legs and holds it in the crook of his elbow as he pushes his cock back inside me.

"I don't know if I can come again after that."

Trent just smiles at me as if I'm adorable for thinking he can't get me there a second time. Though if we are being technical about it, it would be the fifth time total of the night. Five orgasms. One night. Hell, one hour. I want to cry with relief at the knowledge that my body can do this. It can bring me pleasure. It can bring someone else pleasure. There is nothing wrong with my body, despite the lumps and rolls.

"Get out of your head, woman," Trent growls in my ear. "The only thing you need to think about right now is my cock wringing every bit of pleasure from your sexy body. You look at me. Only me. And keep those beautiful eyes open. You got it?"

"Yes."

As impossible as it seems, Trent makes good on his word. My second orgasm from his cock alone comes while he is banging me against the wall, sweat dripping down his face and chest. I don't know why I decide to lick it off his skin, but when I do, the salty flavor of him bursts across my tongue, and I can't get enough. I'm sucking his neck, clawing at his back, and that is when I come undone.

The third comes back on the bed. He holds my ankles in the air, crossing my legs so that I go even tighter around his dick. He roars and swears, says he refuses to come even once until I come on his cock one more time. The intensity of the position makes me delirious, and more quickly than I thought possible, I'm screaming my head off again.

Somewhere in the middle of the screaming and thrashing and coming, Trent pulls out of me, and I whine in protest, my whole body feeling empty without him inside me. But then his hand pumps up and down quickly on his cock two times, my juices glistening on his shaft. With a yell so feral I'm truly afraid for a moment that he is going to turn into a caveman right before my eyes, Trent spurts long warm ropes of cum all over my chest and belly, and even a little on my chin.

Fuck. No condom. We didn't use a condom. I didn't even think about it. I was so wrapped up in the amazing sensations that I totally forgot about the stash of condoms in the dresser drawer.

Thank God he remembered to pull out.

***

"I think you killed me." I half laugh, half pant the joke from our collapsed position across the bed.

The whole thing shakes with Trent's deep chuckle. "I don't think it's possible to die from coming too much, but it was my pleasure to test it out for you."

One of my legs is draped over his thigh as we both lie on our backs, his arm tucked around my shoulders, fingers caressing up and down my arm. I hadn't expected this from tonight. I knew we would most likely have sex. I hoped it would be good. But this intimacy after is kinda throwing me for a loop.

Shouldn't he be pulling on his pants and heading for the door? But he's just lying there, as if he has no plans to move for the rest of the night.

Suddenly the awkward moment crashes down around me. What do I do? Ask him to leave? Say thank you? Is there a politeness protocol for one-night stands? I really have to pee. Am I allowed to get up and pee? Or do I have to wait for him to go so he doesn't have to think about my bodily functions when he looks back on this night?

"Woman, would you stop squirming around? I need to sleep for, like, ten minutes, then we'll go again." Trent rolls over, throwing his arm around my torso and pulling me in tight to his chest.

What. The. Fuck.

Again?

We just screwed for over an hour straight. I glance at the Hello Kitty clock on the wall my sister gave me as a housewarming gift. No, an hour and a half. No way can he go again after that.

Shit. I *really* have to pee.

Jumping from the bed, I stumble over my own damn feet, bumping my shin on the end of the damn Murphy bed. Double shit, did I just give him a perfect view of my ass when I fell over? What the hell am I thinking? He just stared at my ass for an hour as he drilled me from behind.

"Where are you going?" he calls after me as I damn near sprint to the bathroom on the other side of the kitchen. I don't bother answering.

I need to call Meg. She can tell me how to get this guy out of here. I mean, he is super nice, and hot as sin, and amazing as all hell in bed. But this is one night, and it needs to stay one night. So, he needs to get the hell out of Dodge.

"Phone, phone, phone. What did I do with my phone when we got here?" Pacing back and forth in my tiny bathroom is kind of pointless. Step, step, turn; step, step, turn. There is nowhere for me or my rising panic to go. Finally, the need to relieve myself is too much to ignore, even while in the middle of a panic attack. I sit down on the toilet, and it rocks back and forth the way it always does.

"Francie, your phone is on the floor where you dropped your purse."

Triple shit. The guy I just banged cannot listen to me pee. I may not know much about casual sex, but I know that listening to the woman you met less than three hours ago and have already given multiple orgasms to pee is not sexy.

"You want to open the door and tell me what's going on? Then I'll hand your phone over."

Could this get any more embarrassing? Holding back the pee is starting to hurt, but I will be damned if I am going to release the floodgates while he is standing on the other side of the door. "No. Just leave it on the floor, and you can go now."

A deep rumbling chuckle vibrates through the door. "Honey, I'm not going anywhere until you open this door and talk to me."

"No talking necessary. You fulfilled the job description as it was posted on craigslist. Big dick, check. Awesome sex, double check. There is really no need to stick around." I try to keep my voice light and carefree. As if this is no big deal. Fucking a man until I nearly pass out and then panicking as soon as it is over is totally normal. La-di-fucking-da. But the panic is easily recognizable even to my own ears.

"Listen. Why don't you finish up in there. I'll grab us some drinks from the fridge, and we can relax and talk for a while." I can still hear the damn smile in his voice. The fact that he finds me so damn amusing is really starting to piss me off. No. Don't think about pissing. No waterfalls. No trickling water.

"Oh my God, will you please just walk away from the door so I can pee without you hearing?" Sometime during my rage spiral of shame, I let loose and start peeing, at the exact same time I hear the heavy footfalls of Trent walking away.

He absolutely heard me pee. Damn it all to hell.

I stall for as long as I can after cleaning up, even going so far as to brush my teeth. But I really can't stay in the bathroom all night. I have a feeling Trent is a patient man and totally willing to wait me out on this one. Why didn't I bring a robe or shirt or undies or anything to cover up with in here with me? I don't even have a towel because it is laundry day, and they are all sitting folded in my laundry basket.

Gathering the last shreds of my dignity, I march out of the bathroom butt-ass naked to find Trent sitting up in the bed, his back propped up against the wall, and one of the manuscripts I've been working on in his hand. And he is hard. Like, really hard. Pointing straight to the ceiling and twitching hard.

I quickly grab his shirt from the floor and slip it on, needing one of us to be clothed for what is surely going to be a hell of an awkward postsex talk.

"So, did you write this? Because, holy shit, I volunteer to be a guinea pig to test out some of these scenes." Trent flips the page, not taking his eyes off the manuscript.

"No, I don't write them, I edit them." I have no clue what to do right now. I can't sit on the bed with him, that's weird. We just had sex on that bed. There is a wet spot somewhere on that bed with cum from both of us mixed together. Strangely, I find the idea hot and not at all gross.

He lays the manuscript down on the floor beside the bed, his brow lifted in curiosity. "How'd you get into that?"

"Ummm, a few years back a friend of mine from high school wrote a romance novel and asked me to look at it because she remembered what a freak I was for grammar." I look everywhere but at Trent. Looking in his eyes feels dangerous right now, as if by making eye contact with him I will start catching feelings. I don't need feelings for this hot Adonis naked in my bed. I came down with a bad case of feelings when I was a teenager and ended up wasting half my life. No, thank you. No more with the feelings. "It was her first book, so she didn't have the money to spend on an editor. She paid me fifty bucks to read and edit her manuscript. Then she told some of her writer friends, and they all started coming to me too. I got so busy I had to raise my rates to scare some of them off. But then my friend hit it big. Like, really big. She keeps me on retainer now, and I still take other clients. It was thanks to those books and those writers that I grew a spine and left my husband. I realized there was better out there, that our relationship wasn't good or normal."

"Good for you. That is pretty amazing." Unable to avoid it anymore, I glance at Trent and find his eyes burning with lust and something else that I don't want to touch with a ten-foot pole. Something like feelings. "Why are you standing there? Come here. I want to try out this scene from the book."

"I mean, aren't we done now? We had sex, and you rocked my world. Good job, by the way. Don't we go our separate ways now?" I take a couple steps toward the bed, stopping when my shins press against the cold metal frame. "This is my first foray into casual sex, so you have to tell me what to do next here."

Trent leans forward, grabbing my wrists before I can shuffle back again. The squeal comes out of my mouth before I can stop it, and before I know what happened, I'm cradled in his lap with my hands pinned behind my back.

"There are a lot of different ways to do casual sex. Sure, you can do the one-night hookups, but really, why would you restrict what just happened here to one night?" Trent pulls one of his hands out from behind my back, shifting both my wrists into the other's grip. "I know your original intention was for this to be one night, but I think the smarter thing to do here is to take advantage of my complete obsession with your body, with your pussy, and use me as your guide."

Gently, his fingers trace my collarbone. They glide over the cotton covering my breasts and sink down to my

44

pussy. He spears two fingers deep into my core, and I writhe, not sure whether I can take any more tonight. Truthfully, I'm a little sore after all the orgasms. But Trent seems to have some sort of vagina voodoo going on, because after just a few strokes, I'm dripping once more and practically begging for him to shove his dick inside me.

"Sure, you could find a new big dick every time you want to get laid, want to try something new. But why bother when you have one that already knows how to make you come apart within seconds?" Trent says all this as if it means nothing to him, as though he doesn't actually give a shit whether I take him up on his offer. But something under the bravado contradicts his tone, a tension that I can tell he is trying to bury.

With his fingers inside me, slipping and sliding in the wetness he is creating, his words make sense to me. Why would I find another guy? This one is so amazingly fantastic in bed, and nice and funny out of it. I would be dumb to pass up this guy's offer to be my sexual tutor, right? "I don't want a relationship, Trent. I need to make that clear. Even when your fingers are doing everything they can to make . . . Uuunmphh." The most unattractive sound possible gurgles out of my throat as he twists his wrist and does something with his fingers inside me to make everything else seem completely unimportant.

"Shhh, don't you worry, girl. I know exactly what this is." There is too much significance laced in everything he says. Too much awe in his eyes as he looks at me.

But I'm having a damn hard time caring at this point, not when yet another orgasm is building and growing inside me.

Just as I'm about to start screaming my freaking head off again, Trent slows everything down, easing his touch to a barely there whisper. "This time, I'll take you slow. Show you that a fast, furious fuck is incredible, but a slow build to the cliff can be just as amazing. You'll beg for me to let you come, but when you get close, I'll back off. You don't have to worry, though. When I finally let you dive over the edge, you'll thank me."

Holy fucking shit. What have I gotten myself into?

CHAPTER SEVEN
Trent

"Dork. I know you said not to come over before nine anymore, but come on, you know I couldn't wait to hear about last night."

A strange woman's voice echoes through the tiny apartment. She really doesn't need to shout to be heard in this place. Before the vestiges of my postsex marathon sleep can be fully wiped away, a short, athletic woman with hair so many different colors I'm not sure which one to focus on first steps into the living room. Bedroom. Well, the room.

"I brought coffee, so you can't be too mad. But I have to know, did the mountain man give you a deep dicking to remember?" Whoever this lady is, she's not watching where she is going, instead looking at her phone and sipping from a Starbucks cup.

I huff out a laugh at her crude language, so unlike the woman whose breasts are pressed against my side. "Well, I don't mean to brag, but I'd like to think it was a pretty damn deep dicking."

Rainbow Brite, as I've decided to call her, stops in her tracks, eyes round with shock. But the shock doesn't last long. She smirks and leans against the wall. "Hellooo,

Mountain Man. I'm surprised you're still here. FranFran was adamant that this would be a wham-bam-thank-you-ma'am type of situation."

"Well, to be fair, she tried." I glance down at the beauty wrapped around me, flashes of the night before inundating my senses. "But I can be very persuasive."

"Yeah, I can imagine, given the size of the tent your morning wood is popping right now."

Shit. In my exhausted state from the four . . . no, five . . . rounds we went last night, I completely forget we are lying here with nothing but a thin sheet covering us. The combination of nature and boobs pressed against me has the old tripod at full effect. Bending one knee up, I try to hide exactly how happy I am with my current position.

"So, do you want me to have Francie call you?"

I pause, waiting for this over-the-top girl to fill in the blank.

"Meg. The sister." The amusement on her face slides away, revealing a more protective emotion in its wake. "Listen, Mountain Man, Francie has been through a lot. More than she probably let on."

Despite the wacky hair and short stature, this girl is actually intimidating me a little right now with her glare and suddenly stiff stance.

"She is just starting to be able to stand on her own, and she doesn't need another man coming in, trying to railroad everything in her life."

I open my mouth to say something, but Meg holds up the hand holding her phone to silence me, barely even pausing to take a breath in the middle of her diatribe.

"I'm sure you have the best of intentions. Fran is sweet. She's insanely smart. And just about everyone but her knows how gorgeous she is without even trying."

I can't argue with that point.

"But she also has trouble standing up for herself. You were obviously able to bowl her over last night, because she had no plans to let her first foray into casual sex stay the night. So, if your plan is to find some weak woman who you can lord over, just get out now. I'm not standing by and letting my sister go through that shit again."

By the end of her speech, Meg's face is red, and she's huffing a little with indignation. But strangely, I don't mind. It warms something inside me to know Francie has someone like this in her life. Someone who will fight the battles Francie might not be able to yet. I hope I will be given the same chance to help protect the beautiful woman in my arms. Eventually. I know that spot will need to be earned, not taken.

"I promise I have no intention of being some dictator in her life." I glance down at Francie's sleeping face. Her cheek is kind of scrunched up against my chest, there is a thin line of drool running onto my side, and her hair is a massive tangled nest of curls, but damn if she isn't the most beautiful thing I've ever seen. "But I also don't want to be a wham-bam-thank-you-ma'am type of situation. Maybe that was the intention, but after spending one night with her, I know it won't be enough." Tearing my eyes away from Francie, I slide my gaze back over to her sister, who has lost some of her angry edge. "She told me some of what she had to deal with during her marriage. I'm willing to jump through whatever hoops Francie feels the need to put in front of me to trust that I won't be the same as her ex."

"Even if one of those hoops is letting her be with other men?"

Before I can formulate an answer to that question, Francie moans, stretches her legs out next to me, wiggles around a little, and the space between her eyebrows scrunches up in confusion.

Slowly, she pulls one eyelid open, sees me, and then both her eyes go wide with surprise. "Holy shit. That happened. You're still here. You heard me pee."

Fuck, she is adorable. Could I do it? If Francie said she needed to sleep with other guys before settling down again, could I be strong enough to stand by and watch her play the field, hoping she would come back to me in the end?

I honestly don't know.

"He heard you pee?" Meg laughs hysterically at the foot of the bed, almost spilling her coffee all over the floor. "What the hell kind of kinky shit are you into now?"

"Meg!" Francie sits up, forgetting her nakedness for a moment, the sheet slipping down around her waist and exposing those delicious tits. If my cock hadn't already been saluting her, it definitely would be now. She scrambles to cover herself before laying into her sister. "What are you doing here? How long have you been here?" Her eyes shift to the cup in her sister's hand. "That better be for me."

Chuckling to myself, I lean over to kiss Francie's bare shoulder. "Why don't I go use the facilities while you two talk. Meg, could you turn around so I can pull some pants on?"

"I suppose." The strange woman turns on the spot, but before I can stand from the bed, Francie grabs my arm.

"Not in front of the mirror, Meg." Francie's chastising tone has me laughing as I look over to see her sister winking at me in the mirror.

"Hey, can you blame me?" This time, she really does turn so she can't see me in all my glory.

I pull on my pants from the night before, skipping the underwear since I can't figure out where it ended up, and stride toward the bathroom on the other side of the apartment. "I'll just get cleaned up, then I'll take you ladies out to breakfast."

"Oh, no, you don't have to do that."

I look back over my shoulder, and my breath completely leaves my lungs at the vision behind me: Francie, sitting up on the bed, the sheet pulled up to cover her breasts, her hair in what can only be described as a very dark lion's mane, and little bruises all over her collarbone, left from my mouth.

"I can make breakfast here instead if you want." Please don't let them pick that option. I have no clue how to cook anything more complicated than cereal.

"Pfft, with what?" Meg looks as if she wants to bust out laughing. "Unless you want Easy Mac for breakfast, you aren't going to have much luck in this kitchen."

Francie tosses a pillow at her sister, who ducks out of the way but spills some of the coffee on the floor.

"That settles it then. Breakfast is on me." I don't even give them the chance to answer, just turn and walk to the tiniest bathroom I have ever seen in my life. Seriously, my pantry at home is bigger than this thing.

As I discovered last night while Francie had her little freak-out, this place has no insulation, allowing me to hear pretty much everything being said between the sisters in the next room.

"He seems nice. Hot." I can hear a note of teasing in Meg's voice, and I really hope she isn't going to give Francie too hard a time about this.

Something squeaks. Maybe the springs in the bed as Francie gets up? Or is her sister sitting down? You really can hear everything in this place. I run my hands over the plaster in the bathroom, making a mental note to check up on the landlord for this place. There are so many code violations I can't even list them all.

"He is nice." Francie's voice is harder to hear, quieter. But nice is good, right? "Last night was incredible. But I think he might want more."

"Would that be so bad?"

There is a long pause, and I feel as if they might be doing some weird sisterly nonverbal communication. I don't know. Now I also feel like a jackass, eavesdropping on the girl I just offered to be a sexual tour guide for.

Trying to tune out the rest of their conversation, I take my time pissing, wash my hands, and borrow Francie's toothbrush. I figure I've had my mouth on every intimate place of her body, so sharing a toothbrush is no big deal.

Once I finish up, I open the door and make a big deal about stomping around so they know I'm coming out.

"Okay, what do you say? Pancakes?" Once I round the corner of the slap of Sheetrock this place laughingly calls a wall separating the kitchen from the living space, I see Francie is dressed in yoga pants and a slouchy shirt that hangs off one shoulder. Fighting every instinct to get down on my knees and praise the person who invented yoga pants, I plaster a smile on my face and go in search of my shirt. "There is this place just a few miles away that has all these wacky flavor combinations for pancakes. Apple cheddar, mint julep, lemon pomegranate. I have a feeling you two will love it."

Meg and Francie share a look. One of those looks that make everyone else feel as if they are on the outside looking in at something they want to be a part of. I can see a little bit of panic in Francie's eyes, but before she can open her mouth, Meg pipes up.

"That sounds awesome. Let's do it." She has this big shit-eating grin on her face, and I know this wasn't something they had agreed upon earlier. But I'm not one to look a gift horse in the mouth. I'll take every spare minute with Francie that I can.

"Okay, ummm, just let me get cleaned up." Francie disappears into the bathroom, and once again it is just me and her weird sister.

There is a lot I want to say, but I know Francie will hear everything through the walls, and don't want to tip my hand too early. Last night I told Francie we would keep this as a casual, regular hookup. I would help her discover all the different ways sex can be fun. And I'm going to follow through on that. But I have my own agenda as well. It is now my mission in life to make Francie . . . shit, I don't know her last name . . . fall in love with me. Because I can already tell it is going to be a quick trip down the rabbit hole on my part.

"Um ... Trent ..." Francie breaks the awkward silence, and I am all too happy to run over to where she stands outside the bathroom, holding up her toothbrush. "Did you use my toothbrush?"

"Yeah, I figured it wouldn't be a big deal. I mean, my mouth spent hours between your thighs last night. A little shared toothpaste is no big deal." I walk closer, wanting to back her up into the tiny bathroom and find some new inventive positions to contort ourselves into before leaving for breakfast.

"Wait, hours? He spent hours going down on you? You should be buying him breakfast." Meg is now standing behind me, her jaw on the floor and eyes bugging out, staring at her sister.

Francie is getting all fidgety in front of me, the toothbrush question now a thing of the past. "Is that not normal? Don't a lot of guys go down on girls for a long time?"

"Ummm, no, hon. The good ones go downtown for a little while if you blow them first. The great ones do it without the BJ first. A guy going down on you for hours and not complaining ..." She turns to me. "Did you complain?"

"No, definitely not."

"He growled when I tried to push him away."

"Holy shit. How did you put up one craigslist ad and walk away with a fucking unicorn?"

I kinda feel bad for her sister. If she is this shocked by my absolute craving for Francie's pussy, she obviously hasn't been with the right kind of guys.

"At least tell me he sucked at it. I mean, he was at it for hours. Is that how long it took him to get you off?"

Okay, no one calls into question my pussy-eating game. I'm just about to let loose and tell this girl what-for, when Francie comes to the rescue.

"No! It was incredible. I pushed him away because I thought I was going to pass out from how many times I came." Francie lowers her voice to a whisper and steps closer so she stands with her back to me, as if I can't hear her now. "We went five rounds last night. I'm talking I had more orgasms in the last twenty-four hours than I had in the entire length of my marriage. Did I go from zero to hero? Am I going to be ruined for all other men?"

Fuck, I hope so.

"Wait, you went five rounds last night?" Meg peeks around Francie at me with this amazed, and maybe hungry, look in her eyes. "But, he was popping a tent when I got here. Are you telling me he went five times last night and was still able to get it up this morning?"

"I mean, but that is just nature, right? All men get hard in the morning. Right?" Francie looks back at me for confirmation.

Really, all I can do is shrug, because, yeah, most mornings I wake up with my dick ready to go, but not every morning. "This morning was probably twenty-five percent nature, seventy-five percent your boobs."

"I know, right? I tell her all the time her boobs are magnificent, but she just rolls her eyes." Meg gives me this exasperated look, and I can't help but laugh.

"Can we please not discuss my tits right now?"

"No, right, absolutely return to talking about my cock." This whole thing is by far the strangest morning after I have ever experienced. But in an awesome way. I want more of Francie and her weird questions, her weird sister, and her weird life in general. I'll take it. All of it.

"Fuck, right. Sorry." Francie slips into a pair of flip-flops positioned by the stairs leading up from the alley. "Pancakes, right? Let's go." She's all fake enthusiasm and big smiles as she leads us out the alley to the door opening onto one of the busiest sections of the city.

"Pancakes are this way." I grab Francie's hand and weave our fingers together. She tries to pull away, but that just won't do. Giving her hand a little squeeze, I wink at her and try to show her it is okay. Two fuck buddies holding hands. No big deal.

"So, Trent, what is it you do, other than troll craigslist for horny women?"

"Meg!"

I just laugh, even though Francie is shooting her sister some serious stink eye. "Well, I have a couple things I'm always working on. But right now, my passion is a restoration charity some buddies and I started. We go into houses that have been destroyed because of a disaster and repair them free of charge."

"A charity? Okay, so you are either living on a shoestring budget working at a nonprofit, or you are rich as hell and don't have to work for actual money like the rest of us peons." Meg turns in front of us, walking backwards and not giving a single shit that the people coming the opposite way down the sidewalk have to swerve to avoid her. "Which is it?"

"Oh my God, Meg, that is so rude. Let's play the quiet game until we get to the restaurant." Francie sounds truly embarrassed, which is not necessary at all, so I disengage our hands and sling my arm around her shoulders, giving her a kiss on the top of her head for good measure.

"It's fine, Francie. Don't worry." I turn back to her sister, who has that glint of mischief in her eye again. "I'm not hurting for money. I sold a couple apps and have a tech company that I own, but pretty much runs itself, so I don't need to be in the office every day."

Meg raises one eyebrow and glares at her sister. "He's rich, the Robin Hood of orgasms, and he went down on you for hours. This is when it is okay to get married fast. Seriously tie him down as soon as possible."

"Oh my God." Francie buries her face in her hands, but I just laugh to alleviate the tension. I know Francie is not in a place to think about the long term. I won't comment on how her sister's idea doesn't sound all that crazy to me. I've got nothing but time, and I'll wait as long as Francie needs.

"This is us." I open the restaurant door for both the ladies, laying my hand on the small of Francie's back as she passes me.

As we enter the restaurant, Francie holds me back for a moment, contrition apparent in her eyes. "I'm so sorry, Trent. Meg is a lot to take, especially before having coffee. I know this is the very definition of a weird morning after."

"You underestimate me." Putting my lips right up against her ear, I let all the lust still bottled inside my body make itself known through my voice. "I'd put up with a lot more in order to spend more time with you."

Francie blushes, glances at the ground, and tucks one curl behind her ear. It is such an innocently sexy thing to do that I almost drop onto my knees and beg her to go back to her apartment and not leave that old, creaky Murphy bed for days on end.

But of course, Meg breaks the moment. "Okay, love birds, I was promised pancakes. Stop making goo-goo eyes at each other and sit down."

Francie rolls her eyes, but we both laugh a little at the outrageousness of this situation. For a moment, it's as if we are on our own little team. Trent and Francie against the world. A ball of overwhelming need lodges itself right in my throat. Because I want to be a part of this team for a good long time.

Forever.

I just need to convince Francie of that.

CHAPTER EIGHT
Francie

When we finally part ways after breakfast, I can tell Trent doesn't want to leave. He hems and haws and shuffles his feet but eventually gives in and gives me a scorching hot kiss before walking off toward whatever it is he has planned today.

Thankfully, breakfast hadn't been too awkward. He took Meg's crazy personality in stride, which I have to give him major credit for. But his presence made me feel too much. As we ate, he kept his hand firmly pressed to my thigh, not even wandering north. Not that I wanted him to do that. In a crowded restaurant. With people all around. People who could hear me. Nope, didn't want that at all. He just left the weight of his palm on my leg. And despite wanting more, I liked it. Too much.

I like him too much.

The ad may have been the brainchild of two sisters after way too much wine, but as the dead language says, in vino veritas. In wine, truth. I need to explore my options. Date around. Figure out what it is that I want out of my newly single life. That is what I need to be doing. Instead, I really just want to know when I can see Trent again.

Which is why I need to focus on finding my next

conquest.

"You're insane." Meg kicks her legs over the side of my bed, glaring at me as if I just punched a kitten or something.

"Look, I am not denying that Trent is awesome. In another time and place, I could see maybe trying to pursue something there. But right now, I need to explore. I think I went about this the wrong way. I just jumped straight into sleeping with the hottest man I've ever seen in real life. What I need to do is pull back and just dip my toes into the dating pool. I want to play the field. See what is out there." I scroll through the barrage of emails I got after posting my drunken craigslist ad, hoping to find anyone who looks even half as appealing as Trent. "I just spent the last ten years with a man who I fell too easily in love with, and never questioned that love. I wasted ten years of my life. I'm not making that mistake again. This time I am questioning everything. If I decide to settle down again, which I'm not sure is what I want at all, then I'll know with one hundred percent certainty that I am making the right decision."

"And what if, after all this exploring, you get to the end and discover that Trent was always the right man for you? But you let him get away because you're afraid of making the same mistakes?" My sister looks at me with sympathy. Which I hate. I've had enough looks of pity from people since leaving my ex. I don't need it from her too.

But her words do send a fissure of dread straight to my stomach. The thought of Trent giving up on me, of him finding another woman whom he uses that dirty mouth on, makes me physically ill. Which only steels my resolve to meet other men and find out what else I've been missing out on all these years. I never dated before I got married. Never slept around. No experimentation stage in college. I want all that now.

Part of me wishes I had met Trent later in the game. After I've gotten this itching need to experience the things normal women my age already have out of my system. But then, I'm also thankful that he came first. I needed someone to take control, to show me what my body could do. I can't imagine anyone else taking his place last night. Maybe that is part of the problem.

"Doesn't every woman have a story of the one who got away? It's like a rite of passage." There is no confidence in my voice, and I sound unsure and weak. I hate it. I want to be strong, sure of my own decisions.

"Pfft." Meg hits me with her no-nonsense look that always makes me feel a little bit stupid and a lot naive. "Yeah, lots of women have that story. And every one of them wishes they could go back to the moment you are in right now and make a different choice."

Fuck. I know she's right. But I can't turn back now. I'll always wonder, no matter how good a life with Trent might be. I would always, always wonder what I missed out on. When I think of it like that, it almost seems as if I'm doing this for him. Saving him from getting in deeper with a woman who is not in the right headspace to start something serious.

"Will you just shut up and get the fuck over here to help me pick someone else?"

Groaning, Meg stands from the bed and pads over to my chair. "Here, I made a folder of possible contenders for you." Reaching over my shoulder, she takes control of the mouse and sweeps it around the screen. A folder pops up, filled with half a dozen emails. Much more manageable than the hundreds that clogged my inbox.

"You knew that the whole time and just let me shift through all those freaking dick pics?"

Her shoulders rise up, touching the bottom of her earlobes. "Sorry, chickadee, I'm on Team Trent."

***

Two days later, as I sit in a diner down the street from my apartment, I try to muster up the same level of excitement I had before meeting Trent. But it just isn't happening. Probably because I've already gotten that first time out of my system. I'm settling into the dating scene now. Nerves still zap through my system at the idea of meeting this Joe guy, whom Meg has taken to calling Average Joe.

We talked a few times over email before setting up this date, and he seems like a nice guy. He's an independent wealth manager, which basically means he helps invest rich people's money. The picture he sent me was a headshot he uses on his website. Every strand of his sandy blond hair had been perfectly styled, and he held his head at that weird angle every photographer poses you in for some reason. His eyes looked bored in the photo, but they were a pretty shade of blue that I liked.

The door of the diner opens, and I stand to greet my date. He's a little late, but only by five minutes. Actually, exactly five minutes late I notice as I look at the clock above the door of this fifties-style diner and see the second hand clearing the twelve just as he steps over the threshold. Huh.

"Francine." He comes toward me with his hand outstretched to shake, as if we are meeting for a business lunch and not a first date. "Good to meet you. You're just as lovely as the picture you sent over."

In the end, I hadn't been able to send over the same photo I'd sent Trent. Even the idea had somehow felt like cheating, which was preposterous. One date, a night of insane sex, and daily text messages since the night do not a relationship make. But still, instead of the sexy sweater photo I sent Trent, Joe got a tamer shot from the same photo shoot. I wore tight jeans and a plain white T-shirt that showed just a little cleavage, and I'd been perched on a windowsill with light streaming in all around me.

I take Joe's hand, and instead of shaking it, he pulls it up to his lips, a little faster and with more muscle then I expect, which sends me tripping and almost crashing right into him. Thankfully, I gain my footing before any embarrassing mishaps go down, and he gently kisses my hand, giving me a wink at the same time. Is this supposed to be charming? I find it mostly cheesy and a little disconcerting.

Although, at this point in the night with Trent, I had already been sucking on his tongue, so what do I know?

"I hope you don't mind I went ahead and got a booth and ordered a drink." Sliding back onto the bench seat, I'm a little surprised Joe slides in right next to me instead of on the opposite side of the table.

Joe keeps sliding until I'm backed into the corner and our legs are plastered together from hip to knee.

"No problem, beautiful."

Just as he opens his mouth to say something else, the waitress walks up in her poodle skirt and pink apron. I almost sigh in relief to have someone else to focus on.

"Have you decided what you'd like to order?" The girl looks to be just out of high school and bored out of her mind. Yet some crazy part of me wants to invite her to sit down and chat with us.

I slide the menu over to Joe, but he slides it back and just grins at me. "We won't be ordering any food. Not staying much longer, I suspect."

Um, what?

"Actually, I'm pretty hungry." Ignoring the quirk of his eyebrow as he looks down at my tummy and thighs, I turn to the waitress. "I'll have the BLT with onion rings on the side." Hell, if I could order a side of garlic with that just to get this guy to back off, I would.

The waitress rolls her eyes and slumps her way back to the kitchen.

Okay, I need to regroup. This whole thing started off on the wrong foot. I'm thinking too much about the sexy-man-who-must-not-be-named. Joe deserves a chance. Despite the fact that he did in fact send a dick pic with his original email, he has been super sweet and understanding in our emails as I explained my drunken state the night I posted the ad. And he still wanted to meet even though it wouldn't mean automatic sex. Though when he asked, I said there was still a possibility of sex, depending on how things felt when we met. Now, just having him sit next to me sends a wave of guilt and nausea curling through me.

I try to picture us having sex. But no matter how hard I try, I can't get there. My panties are as dry as if they had just come off the clothesline.

"So, you had a big client meeting today, right? How did that go?"

Joe chuckles a little and leans back a few inches, thank God. "Perfect, as always. I bagged the account. Just the commission on this one guy will have me set for the rest of the year."

"Wow, that's great." I take a sip of my lemonade, searching for something else to say. "And, um, I think you mentioned you like sports in your email as well."

"Well, I have fifty-yard line season tickets for the Steelers, so what does that tell you?" He puts his arm behind my back on the top of the seat and puffs his chest out as if what he just said is a huge deal.

"Truthfully, I have no knowledge of sports at all. Are those good seats?"

Apparently deflated by my lack of enthusiasm about his seats, Joe's shoulders slump slightly for just a moment before he launches into an explanation of how much the tickets cost and what he had to go through to get them and how many men would suck his dick to go with him to a game.

I'm kind of zoning in and out of the conversation, honestly, instead tracing the weird boomerang design in the Formica tabletop. Try as I might to stop it, my mind keeps wandering back to my night with Trent and the easy conversations we had while recovering from our third or fourth go-round. Why did everything he said seem so fascinating?

I can almost hear his gravelly voice telling me about his

buddies and their bet about my personal ad.

But then, it isn't my imagination. I do hear his voice, only it's right next to us. My eyes damn near bug out of their sockets as my head whips up to find Trent looking pissed as hell with his fists clenched at his sides and his eyes boring holes into mine. My jaw slides open, and I keep waiting for words to come out of my mouth, but they just won't. I have no words. Because Trent standing there while Joe sits next to me seems all kinds of wrong. So wrong I want to push Joe onto the floor and claim I don't know how he got there. Which is ridiculous. I don't owe Trent explanations. He was a one-night stand that I am maybe thinking about hooking up with occasionally while I see what else is out there. But even that thought seems wrong, and I have to cringe at myself for even thinking it.

"Wow, what a crazy coinkydink." My sister's overacting is unmistakable, and for the first time, I notice her standing just behind Trent. "There I was, walking down the street, and who do I run into, but our old breakfast buddy, Trent. And I thought, 'Well now, we should get a milkshake together for old times' sake.' And he agreed. And now here you are too. Mind if we join?"

Without waiting for an answer, Meg slides into the opposite side of the booth and pats the seat next to her for Trent to take. As he does, my stupid meddling sister takes off her jacket to reveal a T-shirt underneath that says Team Trent right across the chest.

If she wasn't related to me, and my one and true best friend, I would rip that fucking shirt off her and tell her she's not allowed to wear Trent's name ever again. I hate the wave of possessiveness that washes over me. Especially because I damn well know this whole thing is a giant setup for Meg to drive home her point that I should be giving Trent more of a chance. As if she hadn't been harping on that point every hour for the past two days.

"I'm sorry. Who are you?" Oh, right, my date is still here.

"Allow me to make the introductions. This is Meg, Francie's sister. And I'm Trent, the guy who got to her first and ruined her for all the little dipshits like you." Trent leans his elbows on the table hard, almost toppling it into his lap, as he shoots daggers at Joe.

All I can do is groan and cover my face with my hands. This can't be happening.

Joe looks back and forth between me and Trent, putting two and two together pretty quickly, proving that he is just as smart as he apparently thinks he is. "You answered her ad too?"

Trent gives one nod.

"Must not have ruined her as much as you thought if she's here with me." Oh God, never mind. Joe is not smart. He is an idiot.

Trent growls, literally growls, at Joe. We're talking baring his teeth, werewolf-type growl.

"Francine, I think we should get out of here and leave Meg and ... Trent, was it? ... here to enjoy their milkshakes." Joe slides out from the booth, coming to a stand with his hand outstretched for me to take. "I think we both know where this night was headed anyhow. No point in delaying our return to my place."

The hurt that flashes across Trent's face is unmistakable. He really thinks I was going to go home with this douche canoe. Which I absolutely had no intention of doing. But now, if I don't leave with him, Trent will think it is because of him. He'll think he has some claim on me, which he doesn't. I don't want him to. Do I?

Apparently, I'm not moving fast enough for Joe. He taps his foot on the floor, and that one move is so reminiscent of my ex-husband that I can't even pretend to leave with him and not hate myself immediately. "Francine, shall we?"

"No one calls her Francine, asshole. That isn't even her name. It is Francie. That is what it says on her birth certificate and everything." I love that Meg is jumping to my rescue, but I also want to slap her into next week for putting me in this position.

"Joe, I think you should just go without me. I need to have a conversation with these two." I try to make my voice stop shaking, and do a half-decent job of it despite the adrenaline kicking and screaming through my system.

Muttering something under his breath about not knowing why he bothered with a pathetic chubster, Joe turns and stomps from the diner like a two-year-old. Trent makes to go after him, no doubt to shove Joe's ugly parting words back down his throat, but I lay my hand on top of his, stopping him in his tracks.

Just as he turns those anger-heated eyes back on me, the waitress arrives back at the table with my BLT and onion rings.

"Well, my work is done here." Meg taps Trent's shoulder, and they both slide out of the booth. "I'll see you kids in the morning for pancakes."

"Meg, this isn't over. You are going to be hearing from me later." Like she always does, Meg totally ignores my words and blows me a kiss.

Trent barely acknowledges her exit, instead taking the seat that Joe vacated.

I can't look at him. Anger swirls through me, and I want to hang on to that emotion like a life preserver. But I know, deep down in my gut, that the moment I look at him all that anger will fizzle out and raw, hot desire will take its place.

The barest sweep of Trent's fingers across my thigh makes me jump in surprise. Fuck, and just that little touch has me soaking my panties, despite the Sahara Desert state they had been in up until this moment.

Before I can react, pull away, or tell him to go sit on the other side, Trent moves lightning fast and shoves his hand down the front of my jeans. Instead of slapping him like a normal person would, I moan, way too loud for being in the middle of a diner, and lean back to give him more room.

Those thick fingers push aside my panties and part my lower lips. "Who was all this cream for? Did that little prick make you wet? Or is this because of me?" He swirls his fingers in the arousal gathering at my opening, sliding one finger inside me just a little bit. "Answer."

Damn it, why does that low demand make me want to roll over and do whatever he says?

CHAPTER NINE
Trent

"It wasn't for him." Francie's pouty lips separate slightly as she pants through what I'm doing to her sweet pussy. "And right now, I really wish you didn't get this reaction from me, either. You don't deserve this reaction after the stunt you and Meg pulled tonight."

Fuck, that hurts. I know I'm acting like a jealous asshole, but fuck if I can stop myself at this point. Something deep inside me needs Francie to be mine. There has never been another woman in all my time dating who affected me half as much as Francie does. I'm not letting her slip away. I can't.

If I have to crash every date she goes on, fight with her, then use my fingers, mouth, and cock to remind her what we share, I'll do it. I'll do this every night for as long as it takes. Because the last few nights with nothing but a couple texts here and there have been torture. I'm surprised I don't have a bald spot yet from how much I've been tearing at my hair while talking myself out of driving to her apartment and stuffing her so full of my cock she feels it for weeks.

"You may not want your pussy to give me this reaction." I shove my fingers in until my palm rests on her clit, then give that little nub that I love so much a grind. She slaps her hand over her mouth to stifle the moan that little move wrings from her. "But the thing is, your cunt knows better than your brain. She knew her master the moment I laid my fingers on you the first time. That's why she weeps for me. This little pussy cries for me to fill it. And I will never disappoint her, or you."

"Oh God, Trent, this is so wrong, You have to stop." Francie's practically dancing in her seat trying to hold back the orgasm I know is building up just beneath the surface. "Someone is going to see. Someone is going to hear."

She says it as if it's a bad thing, but her pussy tells me different. The moment those words came out of her mouth she got wetter, tighter, her walls undulating with the first signs of her impending climax. My dirty girl likes doing it in public. And I am one hundred percent with her on that.

"So what if they hear? Let the whole damn restaurant hear what I can do to my woman with just my fingers." I'm situated in the booth so that my back is to the rest of the dining room, blocking anyone's view of this hot woman riding my hand. I might like to talk a good game, but in reality, no one but me gets to see this. My lips press against her ear, breathing the dirty words she fucking loves straight into it so no else can hear. "Every man in here wishes they were in my place. They are probably all sitting at their tables across from their wives, hard under the table and ready to fuck. They'd rather be where I am right now. I wouldn't be surprised if they hear you trying to stuff those moans and screams down your throat and decide to come over and watch as I make you come all over this fucking booth. But you'd like that, wouldn't you?"

Francie might shake her head no, but she bites her lower lip and squeezes her eyes closed. I have no doubt behind those eyes she's imagining exactly what I'm telling her. Picturing men standing around and worshipping her with their eyes. The poor woman spent a decade with some idiot who didn't know the prize he had, neglected and tore her down every chance he got. Now the idea of so many men falling at her feet turns her on. But I'll show her the only man she needs kissing the ground she walks on is me.

"Show them, sweetheart. Let them she how fucking gorgeous you are when you come all over my hand. Show me. I'll never get tired of this show. Never. I'm going to be fingering you to climax in restaurants all over this fucking town for years to come."

Pivoting my hand around, I add a third finger in her tight pussy, then press my thumb directly down on her clit. Her mouth gapes open in a silent scream, and I know from our fuckfest the other night, in a fraction of a second, she'll be unable to hold back her sounds. But despite my words, those cries of ecstasy are for me alone. I capture her mouth in a soul-searing kiss, my tongue mimicking the movements of my fingers inside her pussy. Each sound she makes fills my mouth, and I swallow it down, taking her pleasure deep inside me.

I gentle my thrusts, just petting her inside as she comes down from the intense pleasure. Fuck, I love the way her face goes all relaxed and serene right after a stellar orgasm. As if every care in the world has been lifted from her shoulders. I want to help her unwind like this every single night.

The awareness creeps back in, making her whole body tense bit by bit. I hate it. I want her back to the puddle of sensations I just saw. But she shoves and tugs at my arm, trying to dislodge my hand from her pussy. I'm not a complete asshole, so I let her, bringing my fingers up for a taste of her sweet juices. "Mmm . . . this place has the best desserts."

Warring thoughts play out on her face: complete arousal as she watches me lick my fingers clean, and anger.

"Fuck you, Trent." Francie slaps my arm, pushing at me to get out of the booth. I don't want to, but I also don't want to make a complete scene in the restaurant.

I'm barely standing before she practically falls out of the booth, rushing for the door. Throwing a wad of cash that will more than cover the bill and tip, I chase after her. I can't let her go. Even though I know she wants me to, I just don't possess the willpower to give her space.

For such a short woman, Francie sure can walk fast. By the time I make it out the door, I have to jog to catch up with her half a block away. "Francie, just talk to me. Please."

"Oh, now you want to talk?" She flings around, rage and some other emotion I can't quite place, maybe embarrassment, painted on her face. Coming at me like a pissed-off cat, she pokes me right in the middle of the chest. "You are just like my ex. He manipulated me by tearing me down and verbally abusing me. You are apparently going to do it by using own body against me. You can't fingerfuck me into submission every time you don't get your way."

Is that what I was doing? It is impossible for me to feel like a bigger douche bag at this moment. Never in all my life have I felt as unworthy as I do right now. I don't deserve this girl. And I'm losing her, right in front of my face.

The self-pity lasts a total of thirty seconds before I straighten my spine, ready to take on this challenging woman.

"You know what, fuck it. Yes. I used your body to get you to see reason. I will use every fucking weapon in my arsenal if it means having you by my side." Taking two steps, I get right up in her face, bending down a little to meet her eye to eye. "You're scared of the connection we have. I get it. Your first experience at love and relationships was shitty and left you questioning the voice inside you that is saying I'm the guy for you. But when our bodies meet, it is fucking magic. I've never felt anything like it, and I know you haven't either. So yes, I am going to use that very powerful weapon in the war for you to open your heart to me. I'm in this, one hundred percent. Get fucking used to it."

I grip her face between my hands and haul her lips to mine. At first, she fights me, even scratches my forearm a little. But then she latches on and moves those talons to the back of my head, holding me tighter to her. Our bodies are melded together, shifting and rubbing against each other seeking relief. Kissing my way down her neck, to that secret spot that makes her knees give out a little, I look around best as I can for a place to take her. Just a few steps away there is a dark alley, away from prying eyes. Before she can protest further, I whisk us back there, pressing her back against the wall and devouring her mouth.

My hands work at her jeans, unbuttoning them and shoving them down her legs. She whimpers and moans into my mouth, and I growl as I shove my hand up her shirt to grab one fantastic breast. Her hands work at my pants, undoing the belt and button quickly, no shaking hands this time. Once they open, she wastes no time taking my dick out and working it up and down, as if she's been doing it every day of her life.

That tight little hand with the stranglehold on my cock brings me to the edge far too quickly, and I stop her before she makes me blow my load all over the sidewalk. Hell no. When I come, I will come deep inside her. No place else. Gripping both her arms, I spin her around, pressing her chest against the cold brick building.

"You naughty girl. You hiss and spit at me like a kitten, but all the time you're just fighting against what you really want. I know it. You know it. And I'll remind you of it every day until you accept that I am your future." I line my dick up with her dripping pussy and drive home in one thrust. "Tell me, kitten, tell me how much you love my cock inside you."

The mewling whine falling from her lips turns me on

so hard. Now that I'm inside her, she's gone all soft and compliant. "I love it so much. Why do you feel so perfect?"

"Because I'm your god. Damn. Man, whether you like it or not." I punctuate each word with a snap of my hips against her soft ass. "This pussy was built from me. I know what you need, and I'm not afraid to give it to you." I pull out until my dick almost falls from her wet, warm sheath, then shove back in before that can happen. "I'm fucking you in the middle of the city, steps away from people going about their business, like a little slut. But you're my slut. No one else gets this pussy. You understand me?"

She doesn't answer, too busy biting down on her lip to hide her reactions. A churning starts up deep in my belly. I know she was right before. I can't fuck her into spending her life with me. And that knowledge strikes fear in my heart as I've never known. I don't know any other way to get through to her though. So, I'll use what I know about her body, her newly discovered kink for public sex. And tomorrow, I'll keep talking to her. Keep being there for her. Even if she continues to see other men, which makes me want to yell and tie her to my bed. But I'll do it. Because I know, at the end of this tunnel of confusion and fear she's in right now, I'll be the one on the other side, waiting to spend our lives together. She doesn't know it yet, but I'm as stubborn as she is, and I'm not giving up.

Dispensing with words for the time being, I let our bodies communicate for us: the slap of our bodies meeting echoes in the alley, panting and moaning escape even after I clamp my hand over her mouth to quiet them. It doesn't take long for her second orgasm of the night to come fast and hard. Her whole body shakes in my arms as the pleasure bursts inside her. She bites my hand, and for some reason, that sting of pain is what sets me off, coming harder than I ever have before, straight into her pussy. Some hidden, calculating part of me wishes she were off birth control, that I could get her pregnant right now so she would be forced to stay with me for our baby's sake. It is a sick thought, I know this, but that doesn't make it any less hot.

After every aftershock subsides, I pull out of her tight pussy, groaning and growing hard again when I see my cum drip from her used hole. It is the most beautiful thing I've ever seen. Slowly, I bend to pull her jeans back up her legs, redressing her as she slumps against the wall, totally spent. Once we are both decent, I sweep her into my arms in a bridal carry.

"No, I can walk. I'm too heavy for you to carry." Her voice is weak, and there isn't a force in this world that could make me put her down.

"Stop it. Let me carry you. Let me take care of you." I'm not ashamed to admit my voice cracks a little at the end, my emotions raw and on the surface after the fucked-up night we've had. "Please, let me care for you."

Francie's only response is to lean her cheek against my shoulder, nuzzling into the spot that feels as if it were made for her. I walk the five blocks to her apartment building, and she doesn't even notice when I unlock her door with my own key. Or the newly upgraded security door and cameras in the alley. She'll find out tomorrow she has a new landlord.

CHAPTER TEN
Francie

My mind has been running nonstop since the alley incident, as I've started calling it. I'm so confused I'm starting to question every single decision I make. Oatmeal or Cheerios for breakfast? Well, oatmeal will keep me full longer. But the cereal box says Cheerios are heart healthy. My heart has been hurting lately. Maybe I should go with that? I can do with some heart healing right about now. Though I don't think the makers of Cheerios intended for their tasty little Os be the cure for a mixed-up heart.

It has been a week since my disastrous date and subsequent alley sex. After carrying me home, Trent and I silently cleaned up in the shower together, then crawled into bed and fell asleep within minutes. Sometime in the middle of the night, we both turned to each other and had the most intense, quiet sex. Words weren't needed, only the slide of bare flesh against bare flesh. It felt like making love. But that scares the ever-loving shit out of me, so let's just stick with sex for now.

Since then he's texted me every single day, sometimes jokes and memes, sometimes asking about my day. My first instinct was to text back every detail of my day, but I beat that down, instead ignoring the texts or sending short answers. My rapid attachment to this man is petrifying. The last thing I need is to become reliant on another man for my happiness. But he makes it impossible to ignore him.

Meg is no help either. When I try to talk to her about everything, she just tells me to go on another date with Trent. One where we don't end up banging each other's brains out. But I don't need to go on a date with him to know that we would have an amazing time. So much chemistry exists between us I already know a night spent with him would be one of the best of my life, in or out of bed.

There doesn't seem to be an easy answer. I can ignore the pull toward Trent and our invisible connection, continue to date and sleep with other men to satisfy my curiosity. But then I run the risk or hurting and losing Trent, which makes me physically ill. Or I can give in to everyone and everything telling me to run toward this strong man, to hold him close so he can't escape. But that thought brings a different kind of panic. A kind of claustrophobia that grew over the eight years I was stuck in a stifling marriage to a petty man.

But maybe there is a third option. Maybe I can explore my desires and curiosities while also exploring what Trent and I could have together. If there is one thing I've learned from the women I call clients, it is that I don't need to give up who I am to be with the right man. And I truly believe Trent could be the right man.

Which is why I am sitting in a bar, shredding the poor label off my beer. Okay, truth time? I am so nervous I might puke. I've been nursing this beer for the better part of an hour. It is one of those craft brews filled with fruity notes of something or other. I don't know. But it barely tastes like beer, which is why I like it. It took me forty-five minutes to work up the courage to text Trent and ask him to meet me here. I'm going to pitch him my idea.

I'm not sure how he will react.

Just as I take the last sip of my now warm beer, a warm body smelling of sawdust and sweat slides onto the stool next to me. God, why does he have to smell so fucking amazing, even straight off a jobsite? He had wanted to go home and shower, but I insisted he had to come immediately. Otherwise, I might lose my nerve.

"Hey there, angel. What was so important I couldn't even wash the wood shavings from my hair?" There is humor in his voice, but also concern.

I pull as much oxygen as possible into my lungs, getting a little woozy from the pure masculine smell of the man I can't stop thinking about. "I've come to an important realization. You are pretty much perfect in every way. I know I'm an idiot for pushing you away and wanting to try dating other men. The other night with Joe, plus some conversations I've had with other guys online, has proved that you are one in a million. I knew that from the beginning, but I was so stuck in this idea that I shouldn't settle down right after getting divorced. That I should be out there sowing my wild oats or something equally cliched."

The bartender interrupts my diatribe when he drops off another beer for me, even though I didn't ask for it. I must just have that desperation hanging around me that begs for more alcohol.

"Francie, I understand your reasons. I wish I could say I was sorry about the other night, for crashing your date, but I'm not. That guy was a major asshat. He didn't deserve to even sit at the same table as you." Trent sucks in a breath, obviously trying to even out his sudden burst of anger about Joe. His protectiveness makes me smile a little, though I try my damnedest to hide it from him.

"I'm not sorry you showed up either. But Derek, my ex, was the first boy I ever dated, and that turned out to be a disaster. Now, only a year after separating from him, and weeks since officially divorcing, the first man I date is making me want to take that risk all over again. That scares the shit out of me." Finally, I hazard a glance at Trent. It isn't fair that he can look sexy even with paint-splattered clothes, his hair a complete mess, and a smudge of dirt down his jawline. But he does look sexy. I want to drag him to the nearest shower, clean him off, then get him dirty in a totally different way. "Part of the fear is that you will change after we've been together for a while." Trent opens his mouth to say something, but I barrel on, knowing I need to get this all out now. "But a bigger part of the fear comes from the unknown. I've had all these fantasies when it comes to sex, but the two nights with you are the most adventurous my sex life has ever been. I don't want to be old and wish I had experienced more. I want to be one of those old ladies who talk inappropriately about the time she sucked some guy's dick while watching the latest *Star Wars* movie in theaters."

Trent laughs, but I can tell he isn't laughing at me in a mean way but in a she's-so-adorable way.

"So, I have come up with a plan that I think might work. And I'm hoping you will go along with this plan, because there are things I need to explore before I can settle down or be in an exclusive relationship, or whatever the hell adults call the whole being boyfriend-girlfriend thing."

"Okay. Do you want to tell me about this plan?"

The time has come to woman up, gird my loins, and tell this raging hot man exactly what I need from him in order to move forward. Because the reality of the situation is I do want to move forward with Trent. To do that, I have to be embarrassingly honest.

"I want to date you." Trent smiles so big his white teeth almost blind me. "But I also want to see and experience things that might involve other people. I have made a sexual bucket list. Things I've read about. Things I've seen in porn. Things I've fantasized about. I want to explore them. With you. But also date. I don't want this to just be sex. I want to see if we can be more. But I don't want to regret missing out on the things I'm curious about. So, I propose for every normal date we go on, we also check off something from my bucket list. Not necessarily at the same time as dates, but just to keep things even and everything."

The blinding smile Trent had at the beginning of my explanation fades a little but doesn't go away entirely. He seems to be truly considering what I've said. "Okay. I can understand that you want to experience new things. Especially given the nature of your marriage. Um, can I see this bucket list and we can talk about it more?"

With shaking hands, I pull the folded-up piece of paper from my purse. I've been thinking about some of these things for years. Hell, some even before I got married. But this morning marked the first time I ever sat down and wrote them out. I thought I would feel like a deviant once I saw the stark black words against bright white paper. But I didn't. I felt empowered. I am taking control, while also giving in to the possibility of something deeper with Trent. I trust him, even after our short time together. I know he will take this seriously, won't judge me.

Smoothing the paper out, I slide it facedown to Trent, as if it holds the secret code to disable a bomb or something. His fingers graze mine as he takes the paper from me, and I can see him actively trying to hold back a smile playing around the corners of his mouth.

Then he turns it over. Watching his eyes as they skim down the page, I bite my thumbnail, waiting anxiously for his thoughts. The beginning of the list is admittedly pretty tame.

Make out for hours with no sex expectations, sixty-nine, role-play, get blindfolded, phone sex, spanking, masturbate in front of a man, watch a man masturbate for me.

But as I warmed to the idea this morning, the list started going a little off the rails from there.

Get covered in his cum, watch other people have sex in

person, have people watch me have sex, rough sex, anal sex, double penetration, get tied up, tie someone else up, forced submission role-play, learn to deep throat, sex toys, threesome with two men.

Altogether there are about fifty items on the list. They range from the most innocuous things that I assume most people in their early twenties have done, to things I know even my most adventurous of friends wouldn't even consider. But the thing is, I have considered them. Even before starting my editing business, sex always fascinated me. But being a little shy about my body, I never felt comfortable asking for them. The few times I worked up the courage to ask for my ex to come on my tits or to try a new position, he would look at me as if there were something very wrong with my head.

So maybe I'm testing Trent a little. Will he be okay with the list? Help me achieve the items on it? Indulge my wants and needs as much as his own? Or will he shut me down? Will he belittle me for the things I want?

The longer he stays silent, looking at the list, the more I feel like a fool. I'm just about to snatch the paper back and tell him to forget it when he shifts in his seat. His hand disappears from the bar, and I know he's adjusting that giant cock of his. That is a good sign, right?

"Wow." He takes the same hand that just made things downstairs a little more comfortable and runs it over his face. He looks up at the ceiling. Back at the list. Back at the ceiling. Signals for another drink. "I can't decide if I'm happy you did this here, so I can't maul you and cross a few things off the list, or mad because I can't maul you and cross a few things off the list."

"Well, that is why I did it in public. We need to talk about this, not just screw each other's brains out. Though, I'm not opposed to doing that after the talking." I squirm a little in my seat as well, the pulsing between my legs getting stronger from just the knowledge that my list excites him in some way. "So, the list doesn't freak you out?"

Trent laughs a little, his eyes burning with humor and lust. "Freak me out? No. I'm not going to lie. I'm not crazy about everything on here. But most of it I am more than down for."

"What parts are you not a fan of?" I have a feeling I know which items he isn't going to like. But I want to talk through them with him. Explain my reasoning.

"I want to know how rough exactly you want sex. I'm down with a good hard fuck, but I don't want to get too far into pain territory. Also, the forced submission stuff freaks me out a little. We would have to talk about that a lot before we even attempted something like that." Shock must show on my face because he turns toward me with an earnest expression. "My top priority will always be your safety, so that is why those items are first on my list of concerns."

Swoon. Seriously, it feels as if my heart has just melted, along with my panties. "Okay, I don't want pain per se. I just want to be manhandled I guess. A little biting, spanking a little harder than we did the other night." I bite my lip, looking around to make sure no one is listening as Trent takes another sip of his beer. "Um, maybe a little choking?"

Coughing and sputtering, Trent looks at me and his wide, shocked gaze locks with mine, but I can't read what is going on behind those beautiful brown eyes. "Jesus, are you trying to kill me?"

CHAPTER ELEVEN
Trent

I'm not sure it is physically possible for a pair of jeans to strangle your dick, but right now it feels as if my cock has decided to give it a shot. The image won't get out of my head, no matter how hard I try. Me pounding into Francie's pussy full tilt while my hand is wrapped around her pretty throat, not really choking her, just putting a little pressure there, reminding her who is in control.

Goddamn, that is hot. "I can work with that, yeah."

I shift a little in my seat again, trying to give my dick some breathing room, but at this point, nothing is really going to help. Nothing but getting inside Francie.

From the onset of this whole thing, Francie made it pretty clear she was curious about things of a kinkier nature. I mean, she did admit that she sometimes watched gangbang porn, though she insisted that she didn't actually want to experience that. But looking down her list, I realize I underestimated how kinky she truly could be.

"You know, there are things on this list that I haven't done. Things I've never even put real thought into doing."

"I figured. And I don't want to pressure you into doing anything you aren't comfortable with." Francie can't stop fidgeting. The label on her beer is just a pile of scraps at this point, and I'm a little afraid she might bite her thumbnail down to the cuticle. "Is there anything on there that you really don't want to do?"

"I think you know there is. I've never been into sharing my partners, not even ones I didn't have feelings for. The idea of sharing the woman I have a lot of feelings for with another man . . ." Red seeps through my vision at just the thought of another man touching Francie. I don't think I could do that, even for her. "I want to punch whatever hypothetical man would be touching you in the way only I should be."

"I had a feeling you would say that." The disappointment on her face is unmistakable, and I can't help but wonder whether this is going to be a deal-breaker for her. "Would you feel the same way if it was another woman in the three-way with us?"

"Yes, I would." I picture it for a moment: Francie, me, and another faceless woman. I don't feel quite as violent, but it still makes me uneasy even considering someone kissing what is mine. "I'm not going to lie and say I've never thought about what it would be like to have two women at once. It is a spank-bank staple for most men, myself included. But this isn't about the gender of the parties involved. This is about me wanting to be the only person in your life who is bringing you pleasure. The only one taking care of your needs inside and outside of the bedroom."

Francie nods, staring unseeingly at her now empty and bare beer bottle.

"Why a three-way? What about that in particular interests you?" If we hope to have even half a chance of making it together, I need to know everything. Maybe there is a way we can get the feeling of a three-way without having to actually go through with it.

Even during what has to be one of the weirdest conversations I've ever had, I still can't help but notice how beautiful the woman sitting next to me is. Her hair is pulled back in a ponytail, and she's wearing a floor-length flowing cotton dress that is simultaneously sweet and sexy. I'm guessing she doesn't have much makeup on, because a few small freckles are visible across her tan skin. She's all soft curves, and I want to press her up against my hard edges, see how she molds to fit against me in the most perfect way.

After a few long seconds, Francie finally turns to look me straight on. Since I sat down ten minutes ago, she's mostly been avoiding making eye contact, instead giving me quick glimpses before turning back to her drink. But she seems to have gathered her courage and is now diving in headfirst.

"I've read a lot of ménage romance books, and I know I couldn't do a relationship like that, split my affections between two men. But the way they describe being filled up in every way possible, how intense it is, that intrigues me. But it isn't just that." Francie leans in a little more, looking around to make sure no one in this dingy little bar is listening. "But more than that, I want to know what it is like to be worshipped by men. To have multiple men dying to please me, but also wanting to get their pleasure from me. I know, on a psychological level, this particular fantasy probably stems from my marriage and the fact that Derek seemed to not care at all about my pleasure, and really didn't seem to take much pleasure of his own in being with me. Just once, I want to be the focus of all the sexual energy of two men, if only to prove to myself that I'm worthy of that."

Fuck. That explanation nearly wrecks me. I want to argue. Tell her that I can worship her enough for a whole army of men. That I will fill her up in every way possible. That she doesn't need to prove anything to anyone, because she is worth so much. But I know my words aren't going to do much in making her believe. Actions will, however. If this is what it is going to take to make her realize that she is a goddess and men would fall at her feet for even a chance at being with her, then I'll give that to her. I'll give her everything. Even if it kills me.

"Okay. I'll try. For you."

The excitement that lights up Francie's face makes the sinking feeling in the pit of my stomach worth it. I'd do anything to make her this happy every single day. I just wish it was me, and only me, giving her that excitement.

***

After the conversation at the bar, Francie wanted to dive into her list headfirst. Thankfully, not with the three-way. We've been knocking items off the list at an almost alarming pace.

Not that I'm complaining.

Just the opposite. Even the items that I've already experienced are brand new just by doing them with Francie. Hell, sixty-nine has become her new favorite thing, and she asks for it almost every time we're together. Sometimes it is a prelude to sex, and sometimes we just enjoy the oral side of things all night, alternating who gets to come. Even after I've shot a load down her throat, she loves to lick and play with my manhood as it recovers, all while I'm devouring her at the other end of the bed. It somehow feels even more intimate than straight-up sex. We've been working on her being able to deep throat, and fuck, if it isn't one of the sexiest endeavors I've ever experienced.

But as much as I've tried to put it off, I've decided we need to get the whole her-and-two-guys thing out of the way. It's been looming over our heads, just sitting there like a storm cloud that puts a damper on everything. I need to get it out of the way so I can stop worrying and obsessing about it. Give her the experience, hope to God it doesn't turn into her new favorite thing, and move on to concentrating on the two of us.

I've been debating how to handle this whole three-way thing for weeks and decided I need someone I could trust. Someone I could explain the whole situation to and know that he wouldn't be trying to horn in and steal my woman. At first Razor wasn't so sure about participating. I get it. We've been friends and business partners since college, and he doesn't want to mess with that dynamic. But I can be a convincing guy, and he eventually agreed. Group sex isn't new to him. He's a mainstay in the local swinging scene, but he's always kept that part of his life separate from me and the rest of the guys.

Tonight, that changes. Tonight, I'm going to let him touch and be with the woman I now know I love. And it is killing me. I've been trying to visualize it. Picture how happy and excited she'll be. Concentrate on Francie and her needs, but inside, a little piece of me is dying. I don't want to do this. Would never even consider it under normal circumstances.

These aren't normal circumstances. I need to prove to Francie that she comes above all else. Even my own needs and desires. She is always first. Always.

"Where are we going?" Francie bounces up and down in the passenger seat of my SUV, excited that I picked her up for a surprise date. She has no clue what I have planned for the night. I couldn't talk about it beforehand. I need to just do it.

"You'll see, but I promise you'll like it."

Francie must sense something is off with me, because she reaches over and slides her fingers between mine on the stick shift. "Trent, I know no matter where you are taking me tonight, I will love it because you are there. I know I was a little skittish toward the start of our time together, but you've proved there are good men out there by being the best of them."

I admit it, her words soothe me a little, make it easier to do what I'm about to do. Gripping her hand a little tighter, I bring it up to my lips and give her knuckles a soft kiss. Francie doesn't realize the extent I would go to simply to make her smile. But she's learning.

I pull up to the house Razor just finished renovating

and put the car into park. We both sit in silence for a moment. I need just a second.

Raz is a flipper. He got into it after I started my charity and discovered he loved renovating houses. So now he buys them, lives in them while he works on them, and then sells them for an obscene amount of money. This one is different though; he never lived in this house. It was the first time he'd flipped two houses simultaneously. Which is why we chose it as the location for tonight's events. I wanted neutral territory, but not a hotel where people might hear us.

Francie's questioning eyes swing to me, and she gives my fingers a squeeze.

"Let's go, honey. Time to cross another thing off your list." My heart is hammering inside my chest, not with excitement, but dread. It is a slow, heavy thud against the inside of my rib cage.

The door is unlocked, just as we had planned, and I push it open to reveal the scene I spent most of my day creating. The house is dark except for the candlelight lining the walls on every available surface. Large pillows cover the floor in a sort of makeshift bed. My stomach churns as I lead her into the room.

A soft gasp behind me has my skin prickling beneath my shirt. "Oh my God, Trent, this is beautiful. Did you do all this?"

I turn to look at what I know for a fact is the most beautiful woman on the face of the planet. My heart skips a beat when I see the look of awe and emotion on her face, tears brimming along her eyelids. "Well, I had a little help."

With those words, Razor steps out from the kitchen. He's dressed in torn jeans and a muscle T-shirt, his blond hair flopping over his eyes and his feet bare. Francie's gaze swings over to him, and her eyes widen in surprise.

"What's going on?" I don't miss the slight tremor in her voice, but I can't tell whether it is because of excitement, nervousness, or doubt. A stupid part of me really hopes it is doubt.

Razor smirks, something I've seen him do before many times, but now there is a predatory element to it that sets my teeth on edge. Maybe I shouldn't have picked one of my friends. I have a feeling after this I will never be able to look at him again without wanting to rip off every inch of his skin that touched my Francie.

"You must be Francie. Trent has told me a lot about you." Razor takes another step into the room, closer to Francie. His eyes take in every inch of her from bottom to top, and the heat there is unmistakable. But also, a bit of indifference. I can tell he finds her attractive, but that is as far as it goes for him. "And boy, he did not lie when he told me how beautiful you are."

Francie turns back to me. So many emotions and thoughts are scrolling across her face they become a bit jumbled, and I'm not sure what they mean. "Trent, is this what I think it is?"

I nod, swallowing down the pain and trepidation tonight is stirring inside me. "This is your fantasy. Razor is a buddy of mine, and I trust him with my life. I trust him with you. If you still want to try this, he is more than happy to help me make your fantasies come true."

Raz steps up behind Francie, not touching her yet, but standing close enough she should be able to feel his presence against her back. "Tonight is all about you, Francie. What you want."

Since meeting Francie, I have rarely seen her at a loss for words. But right now, her eyes are wide and her lips silent.

"Do you still want this?" I whisper to her, afraid if I say the words any louder she will hear the hope in my voice that she'll call it off. But she closes her eyes, then nods. At first it is a resolute nod, but then it gets a little faster, a little more excited.

Cupping her face with my hands, I pull her into a deep,

slow kiss. Over the few weeks since we met, I've learned all the different ways she likes to be kissed. The gentle glide of lips, the deeper passionate prelude to a good fuck, the dance of tongues as we make out for hours. But this kiss is different from all of them. This kiss is meant to ground us, to remind her that I'm with her no matter what. Our tongues still dance, our lips still glide, and there is definitely passion, but there is also love and stability in the kiss. Things we haven't really vocalized to each other yet. Despite my trepidation about this whole thing, my body reacts to Francie the same way it always does, by getting hard enough to pound nails into framing studs.

The air around us changes, and I know Razor has just stepped up to the plate. I lean my forehead against Francie's, trying unsuccessfully to get myself under control. I'm breathing heavy, like a bull in the middle of the fight for his life. All I see is red, but I can't get myself under control. Until I remember what this is all about. Who it is all about.

Francie.

CHAPTER TWELVE
Francie

I don't know what I had been expecting when Trent picked me up tonight. He's been taking the whole dating thing very seriously. We've gone on the typical dinner-and-a-movie dates, then he's done more elaborate things such as setting up a catered dinner under the stars at the local botanical garden. We've spent nights cuddled on his couch having a movie marathon, going back and forth watching each other's favorite films. He's taken me dancing, to art shows, to plays, and my favorite, to a book reading by a local author.

But he's also been taking the list very seriously, so I really should have at least considered the possibility that tonight would be about my list and not a romantic date. Although I can tell that Trent tried very hard to make this night romantic.

I should be excited. This was my top fantasy. Is. It is my top fantasy. We've talked several times about how it would go, what I want out of it, and why I want it. And each time, I never doubted that I want to be the focus of two men's lust. Guilt always lurks in the background because I know Trent isn't happy about it, and I feel bad. But I spent so many years worrying about someone else's happiness, I need to focus on mine now.

Or at least that is what I keep reminding myself.

Because for some reason, the second Razor—what kind of name is that anyway?—stepped into the room, my stomach sank, and I felt as if I might throw up. But this has been me the whole time, insisting I want this experience. Though admittedly, I hadn't thought about it at all in the past week or two. Everything with Trent is so perfect, he makes me forget everything else.

Trent must sense my hesitance, because he asks whether I still want this. At first, my head screams *no*, the word almost pushing its way out of my mouth. But then I think through all the reasons again. I want to experience something many women haven't. I want to be daring. I want to feel what it is like to be desired by multiple men. Plus, I fucking love watching this on all my favorite Tumblr porn blogs. Like, *love*. I might even follow certain blogs because they solely reblog double penetration videos.

So, with all those things in mind, I give Trent a single, strong nod. I'm sure. I'm doing this. I'm not going to throw up. God, that would so be like me. Throwing up in the middle of my first, and probably only, ménage à trois is one hundred percent something I would do. I stuff all my reservations down and try to fake getting excited about this. I'm sure once we get started and they are both touching me, I'll forget ever having doubts.

Trent gently holds my head still as he leans in for a kiss unlike any other he has given me to this point. I feel everything in the kiss. His devotion. His kindness. His patience. His passion. His love.

And every bit of me responds in like. The love that consumes me during the kiss hits me like a bull taking out an idiot running away from him on some street in Spain. Because I have been an idiot running away from it. Trent has been all in since the day we met. I've been the one hemming and hawing, coming up with more obstacles and hurdles and running as fast as I can from the feelings he so easily brings out in me.

This isn't the way it was when I was eighteen and thought I was in love with an older boy. Holy hell, it is nothing like that. This is more than hormones and a manipulative twat of a teenage boy. This is heart, soul, and mind. He knocks the breath out of me and the sense into me with the kiss.

A warm body approaches from behind me. I had forgotten Razor was even in the room. His hands rest on my hips, and I go still. Not one molecule of his skin is touching mine thanks to my jeans, but even still, it feels wrong. Trent breaks the kiss; his breathing is fast and labored like I've never heard it before in all the high-octane fucks we've experienced together. No, this is the breathing of a man in pain. In anguish. On the verge of panic. And I'm doing it to him. Shame and sadness sweep over me.

What the hell have I been thinking?

Razor's thumbs sweep under my shirt, his rough skin touching mine for the first time.

"Stop!" The word comes out literally the second I feel another man touch me. Because it feels cold and strange and not like Trent. In other words, wrong.

Thankfully, Razor takes my command seriously and steps back immediately. Trent pulls his forehead back from mine and searches my eyes. Tears well along my lower eyelids, obscuring my view of his fucking beautiful face. I know men aren't supposed to be beautiful, but he is, inside and out.

And I'm an idiot. Such a huge idiot. How could he love me when I put him through this? "I'm sorry. I can't . . . I don't want to . . . I thought . . ." How do I explain something like this? How do I tell him I almost made him watch me with another man simply because I was scared of loving him too much, too fast?

"Thank fuck." Trent wraps his arms around me, pulling my face into the crook of his neck, which has always felt as if it belonged to me since that very first night.

I turn to apologize to Razor. I don't know him, but the poor guy came here expecting to get down and dirty with two other people and instead is going home alone. But when I turn, he is smiling at us and backing toward the door he came in through.

"Don't worry, Francie. Everyone has that moment they realize some things are better left to porn stars." He winks at me, gives one of those man nod things to Trent, and leaves without another word.

I bury my face back into Trent's warm, welcoming body and sob without reserve. Somehow Trent maneuvers us onto the pillow-covered floor, cradling me in his arms like the big freaking baby I'm currently impersonating.

"Shhh, it's okay, sweetheart. Don't cry." Trent strokes my hair, shushing and whispering comforting words in my ear, rocking me back and forth. So basically, he's never going to want to fuck me again after this display. "Talk to me, Fran. Tell me what is going on in that head so I know how to reassure you that everything is okay."

"I'm an idiot." On top of everything else, my lungs and diaphragm apparently decide to fight the emotional assault on my body with hiccups. So, I can get only a few words out at a time before my whole body jumps and a loud, unladylike croak emits from my throat. "I just . . . realized . . . that I . . . fuck." I draw in a deep breath, willing the words to come out and my obscene display of feelings to go away. "I love you. I realized tonight I'm in love with you, and I know you are in love with me too. You don't even have to tell me. Look at everything you've done for me. No man would set up a romantic threesome for a woman he didn't love."

I can feel Trent's chest shaking a little, and I know he is holding back his laughter. "Actually, if Razor's accounts of how he spends his free time are any indication, lots of men would set up a threesome for women they don't love."

"Okay, maybe, but I know you did it out of love. I feel

it every time I'm around you. And it scared the shit out of me." I sit up a little so I can see his face, and happiness like nothing I've ever felt wells inside my chest. Because it is right there, plain as day on his face. Love. Relief too, but mostly love. "Yes, I fantasized about all these things for so long, but the truth is, when I picture these things in my head now, all I see is you. The truth is, the few nights we've been apart and I've had to use fantasies to get me off, I picture both men in this scenario as you, which I realize is impossible and ridiculous, and I had to create this whole story line in my head about you having a long-lost twin, and then try not to think about the whole related-to-each-other ick factor. But I couldn't picture another man doing those things to me. I tried to rationalize it away as just not being able to think of who else would want me like you, but the truth is I don't want anyone but you to touch me. The minute Razor touched me, everything about it felt wrong. Oh God, I am never going to be able to look him in the eye again. Would it be okay if I just never had to hang out with your friends so I don't have to face the shame of this night?"

"Honey, you need to calm down. You're doing that nervous, upset babbling thing." Trent laughs, and the rich sound of it helps soothe my frayed nerves a little bit. But just a little. "You have no reason to be embarrassed or sorry. I wish there were two of me so I can fuck you every which way you've dreamt of, because you are right, I love you. So much. I think I have since I first got your emails, first saw your picture. And it just grows and deepens every day. As for Razor, trust me, the next time you see him it will be like nothing ever happened. He'll never mention it again."

Trent's ability to reassure me never fails to amaze me. I can be in a total tailspin of anxiety and neurosis, and just a few words from him bring me back to center. "So, you love me, and I love you. Neither of us wants to be with anyone else in any capacity. This is it for us."

"Welcome to the same page as me. You should stay here a while. Like forever." This is something else I have learned about Trent the past few weeks: he can be a snarky little dork sometimes. Meg and he have gotten into quite a few sarcastic snark-offs over breakfast.

"Does this mean we're in a committed relationship now? Are we going to start having date nights at Applebee's, I'll stop shaving my legs, you'll stop going down on me, and we'll have missionary sex once a week?"

Despite the teasing tone I try to adopt, I really am worried about this. In a lot of ways, I am just as inexperienced and confused as a teenage girl. My only experience with love and relationships didn't exactly leave a good taste in my mouth.

"What is with you hating on missionary? Missionary can be hot. Intimate. Passionate. One of these days I'm going to fuck you in missionary position for hours, make you come more than I ever have before. Then you'll be begging for me to take you old faithful-style." Trent turns me in his lap so I'm straddling his hips, and I can't help but notice the raging erection poking me in the thigh. "As for the rest of that nonsense you just spouted, I honestly don't care where we go on dates, as long as you are with me. I don't give two shits whether or not you shave your legs, as long as they are wrapped around me every night. And I will never, *ever*, stop going down on you. Never."

"Wow. I think you just wrote your wedding vows." I freeze as soon as the words pop out from my lips. Did I really just insinuate we were going to get married? "Not that we're to the whole marriage phase yet. Not that I'm saying we have to get to that phase. I mean—"

"Francie, shut up. I am absolutely marrying you, just as soon as you are ready to take that leap again."

Before I can do or say anything else to embarrass myself, Trent covers my mouth with his, kissing me until I'm breathless.

CHAPTER THIRTEEN
Trent

Finally, fucking finally, every piece of the puzzle has snapped together for Francie and me. Sitting on the floor of a strange house where we were supposed have sex with another man might be the strangest place in the history of couples to declare our love for each other, but I wouldn't have it any other way.

But I also don't want to make love to her here. I want to take her home to my house, lay her down in the bed I'm hoping she will someday call hers as well, and show her how unconventional we can be, while still being a committed couple.

Francie must have the same thought, because she stands abruptly from my lap, reaching her hand down to help me up. Which makes me laugh a little since I would end up just toppling her over.

Without words, we clasp hands and practically sprint back to the car. In a blink, we're blindly stumbling through my house, groping and mauling each other as if we hadn't had sex just the night before. The place is relatively small considering what I can afford, but I always thought my money was better spent going back into the company or my charity. But it is still a four-bedroom house with all the modern amenities with a fantastic view of the river. The first time I brought Francie back here she'd walked room to room with a huge Cheshire cat smile on her face, and I knew she was picturing herself here. How she would change it. Where her things would go. But she wouldn't admit it at the time.

"When I move in, we're putting some colors on these walls. All this grey and white is so not us." She mumbles the words around my lips, not willing to break our connection.

I laugh, because a month ago this girl was still trying to date other men, and now she's redecorating my house. And I love it. I love her, crazy neurosis and all. "You can paint whatever the hell you want. Just promise me you'll walk around naked every day."

"Deal."

"I have something I need to tell you." We're stumbling back through the house, trying to walk and grope each other at the same time. "I'm your landlord."

Francie stops in her tracks. "So, you're the one that's been making all the security updates? Refinishing the kitchen? You know I don't actually need all that, right? I was happy with the way it was."

"No woman of mine is going to walk through a dark alley every night to get to her door." I pull her in tighter to me, not wanting even an inch of distance between us. "I bought that building the day after I met you. I couldn't sleep knowing you weren't safe."

"Wow." Francie's mouth drops open, and I have to wonder if I went too far. "That is the sweetest most psychotic thing I've ever heard. Thank you. Now, fuck me."

By the time we make it to the bed, our clothes have been shed all over the house, and we're both panting and moaning, already on the edge of coming even though we've barely gotten started. I need to slow things down. We have all night. Hell, we have a whole lifetime. There really is no need to rush our first night of forever.

"I have a surprise for you." I lay her down on the mattress, then move to the nightstand where I stashed everything I would need for this particular surprise, though I had planned for this to happen in a few days, not tonight.

"You know what I love, besides you? Surprises." Francie presses her thighs together and writhes around on the bed, all her pent-up need manifesting in a fidgeting sex goddess.

"I had planned to do this after crossing the threesome off your list. I wanted to be able to prove to you that I could make you feel just as good, all alone. But now I just want to give you something you've been curious about."

I place the gift next to her on the bed. Brow furrowed, Francie fingers it slowly. "Are these what I think they are?"

"If you think they're anal beads, then yes, they are." We've experimented a little bit with some backdoor action, but haven't gone further than my pinky in her cute little ass. At first, she couldn't stop giggling whenever I ventured back there. But then I popped my finger in one night while I was licking her pussy, and she fucking detonated. That only increased her curiosity about anal play. I can't wait to claim her ass, and these should help things along nicely.

Francie can't stop staring at them. She picks up the roughly foot-long string of light blue beads and twirls them around. While she's distracted, I kneel on the floor between her legs and dive face-first into my favorite place on earth. Her pussy. As soon as my tongue touches her swollen little clit, Francie's hands fly to grip my hair and pull me tighter against her. I'll never forget that first night when she claimed she couldn't get off like this. Now look at her. My brazen girl is humping my face and coming undone in no time at all.

I let her first orgasm subside before pressing my index finger into her tight pussy and slowly fucking her with it, just keeping her warm and on the edge for what comes next. "Hand me the beads, honey."

Faster than I would think she'd be capable of, considering she's still recovering from her hard and fast climax, Francie whips the beads off the bed and dangles them in front of my face between her thighs. "Be gentle."

Kissing her pulsing little clit one more time, I take the beads from her hand, as well as the bottle of lube that is still sitting by her hip on the bed. "Pet yourself, baby. I want to keep you nice and wet while I get you ready."

Like the good girl she is, Francie reaches down and slides two fingers around her clit, fast then slow, and dips them down into her pussy, then back up to her clit. Never staying in any one area long enough to bring herself to orgasm but balancing right on the edge the way she knows I want.

For a moment, I'm mesmerized by the sight of her playing with herself, and I forget what I'm supposed to be doing. Shaking my head in an effort to refocus myself, I get to work slicking up the new toy with the lube and then squirting a healthy dose of it on her tight back entrance. These beads are designed for beginners. The first few are smaller than even my pinky, so I know she'll take them easily, but by the third and fourth ball they get big enough that I know we'll have to work to get them in. No way will we make it all the way to the last ball, which is an inch in diameter.

"Ready, honey?" I gaze up the curves of Francie's sweet body and almost lose the war with my willpower not to say, "Screw this whole kinky thing" and just get my dick inside her cunt right now. The swell of her soft tummy rises and falls with her labored, aroused breathing. Her huge tits are plumped up between her arms, which are still busy at work between her thighs.

But the thing that really gets me is the complete look of trust and awe in her eyes. Francie has always looked at me with affection and attraction. But now, there is a whole new level there. She's given in to the feelings that have been growing between us for weeks. No longer holding back and hanging on to all those bullshit roadblocks she kept throwing up between us. Now she's all in. Just like me.

Biting her bottom lip, Francie nods and whimpers as I push the first bead into her ass. Her fingers fly in a rapid flutter over her clit, and her hips begin to twitch with the first signs of her next orgasm.

"Don't you come yet, Francie. I want the first time you come with a toy in your ass to be all over my cock. I'm going to fill you up so you scream from the feeling. I know you want to wait for that release until my cock is buried inside you." I push the second bead in, and Francie throws her head back, her eyes screwed shut with the effort of keeping her impending orgasm at bay.

"That's it, honey. Reach that other hand down here, and put one of your fingers in your soaked pussy. Feel how wet you get when I fill up your ass. You like being dirty, don't you, Francie? People look at you and think you're such a sweet, innocent woman. But they don't know that at night you let me fuck this body any way I please. They don't know the kinky plans you think up. I'm the only one who gets that part of you."

"Yes, oh God, I love being dirty with you. Only you." Francie's breathing fast and hard, one finger pumping in and out of her soaked channel, the other circling her clit in rapid little movements.

I push the third bead into her tight little hole and get a little resistance right before it pops into place. "How's that feel, dirty girl?" I ask because I need to know exactly where her head is at, but I can read her body as if I've watched her reactions for years, not weeks. Just as the round bead breaches her back entrance, her hips lift off the bed, and she moans low in her belly. Her fingers still their work in her pussy for just a split second and then go back to their frenzied pace.

"So good, Trent. I want your cock inside me. Now.

Please!"

Dear God, I love hearing her beg for my cock. "Not yet, sweet thing. Can you handle one more?"

She nods and tries to keep still for me. The next bead is slow going, but once it slides in, Francie starts going crazy. She's right there on the edge, but I don't want her going over just yet. I abandon the beads, now half disappeared inside her, and grip both her wrists, pulling her hands away from pleasuring herself. Pinning her body to the mattress, I hover over her, forcing her to look directly in my eyes. "Not yet, honey. Shove it down. You're not coming yet."

A few tears escape the corners of her eyes. I know this is intense for her, and I'm so happy it is just the two of us here. She nods, breathes deep, and somehow staves off the orgasm that has been slowly building inside her.

I can't resist. Even though time is short if I want her to come with me inside her, I need to feel her lips again. I cover her mouth with mine, and her moans grow louder as our tongues dance. Her hips undulate beneath me, looking for any bit of friction to give her what she needs.

Quickly, I force myself to give up her succulent mouth and flip her over onto her stomach. Pulling her ass up into the air, I nearly lose my own tenuous hold on my release at the sight of those blue beads dangling from her tight hole. Without any more fanfare, I shove my cock straight into her hot, slick cunt. And that is all she needs. Her walls flutter and constrict around my cock, trying to milk my cum out of me. But I refuse to let go that fast. Not with only one pump inside her. Hell no. My girl is in for the ride of her life.

I fuck her through the orgasm. She's screaming and clawing at the sheets like the little hellcat I know she can be in bed. Every time I thrust deep inside her, my hips slam against her ass, giving the beads a jolt. I think a second orgasm starts right on top of the other, because her upper body gives out until her chest and face are pressed into the bed, and the only thing holding her hips up are my hands.

I slow my thrusts, not wanting her to be totally spent yet. Almost lazily I push every inch into her still throbbing pussy, then drag all those inches back out, making sure she feels every bit.

Gradually, Francie comes back to herself, her breathing evens out, and she presses up onto her elbows to glance back at me. "Holy shit. Every time I think our sex life can't get better, it does."

"Oh, honey, you ain't seen nothing yet." Banding my arms around her torso, I draw her up so her back is pressed against my chest. I can't go as deep in this position, but every single movement of my hips makes the beads shift inside her ass.

Continuing the lackadaisical pace, I kiss along her neck, suck her earlobe, pinch her nipples with both my fingers, caress every inch of her belly, tits, and neck. I make love to her in the middle of the dirtiest fuck I've ever experienced. Because with us we are both at all times. We are dirty and sweet. There is no separating the two.

"You know another thing on that little list of yours I've been dying to give a try?"

Francie shakes her head and moans as I pinch both her nipples, drawing them straight out from her body, then releasing them so her tits jiggle as they fall back to their normal position. Fuck, I love playing with these beauties.

Gliding my hand up to her throat, I wrap my fingers gently around her neck, not putting any pressure there, just holding her in my hand. "How about a little choking, dirty girl? You wanna give that a go?"

I know she likes the idea even before she responds. Her body tells me exactly what she wants. Those sweet juices of hers that I love to devour drip out around my cock and down her thighs. Her breathing picks up just a little, her pulse beating wildly against my thumb on one side of her neck. Then she nods these fast little jerks of her head, and I have to smile. So eager.

I give her a little more pressure against her throat, nothing that will restrict her breathing even a little bit. But enough so she knows I'm there and not letting go. At the same time, I pick up the pace on my thrusts, giving her some sharp, hard pumps. Her arms snake around behind me and grip my ass, trying to get me even farther inside her.

Snaking my free hand down her body, I slip my fingers between her hot, wet folds, running them down to her entrance where I am stuffing her full, and back up to her swollen clit. "You like me in complete control of your body, don't you? I've stuffed both your holes so full, you can feel every little movement. Now I control how much you breathe too. You'll take everything I give you and not complain one bit. Isn't that right, dirty girl?"

Unable to answer, Francie only moans and tries to grind down on my cock, her whole body vibrating with the strength of the orgasm building inside her.

"Answer me." I give her just a little bit more on her throat.

"Yes, love it," she rasps out.

"I know you do. These juices tell me so, even when you can't answer." I swirl my fingers around my pumping cock, right at her entrance. Any minute now this girl is going to detonate. Her pussy is clamping down on me so hard I'm surprised I still have any circulation left in my dick. Fuck, it feels amazing. Removing my hand from between her thighs, I bring my fingers up to just before her mouth, already gaping open while those sounds I love pour out of her. "Taste how much you love it, honey."

No more prompting is required. Francie leans forward, putting even more pressure on her airway, and sucks my fingers into her mouth. That does it. She's screaming and writhing, her nails digging into the flesh of my ass and her cunt clamping down on my cock, milking me for everything I'm worth.

Before I totally lose myself to the moment, I move the

hand holding her throat between us and begin pulling the beads one by one slowly from her ass. Each one that pops out sends her deeper into her orgasm. As I pull the final one out, Francie collapses onto the bed, and I follow, giving three more hard pumps, emptying my balls straight into her puffy pussy.

We're both breathing hard, and I'm pretty sure I might have blacked out for a couple seconds. I'm lying with all my weight on top of her, my dick still lodged deep inside. I roll to the side, staying buried inside her and gathering her in my arms.

"That was everything and more I could have ever wanted from that fantasy." Francie looks at me over her shoulder, her eyelids heavy and her face relaxed. "I love you, Trent. So much."

"I love you too, my dirty girl."

EPILOGUE ONE
One Year Later
Francie

"Do you think we bought too much?" I lift up the two huge shopping bags, heavy with our purchases, and glance over to Trent, who has the biggest grin on his face.

"No way. I thought we showed enormous restraint. Besides, we are going to need supplies for our three months alone in a hut on the ocean." Trent leans over, kissing me with all his might right in the middle of the sidewalk.

Outside a sex shop.

Once he lets me go, we continue walking toward the parking garage, eager to try out our new purchases.

Our wedding is one week away, and I couldn't be more excited. Every doubt and made-up reason I used to keep him at arm's length when we first met have long since evaporated, leaving behind only love and a confidence in our relationship that grows every day. I've never been this happy in my life, and instead of worrying when the other shoe will drop, I know that it will only get better from here.

Of course, there have been hard times. And more will come, without a doubt. But the key to everything in our relationship is communication. I know I sound like one of those super cheesy relationship gurus who write self-help books, but it is the truth. We talk about everything, whether it's how our days went, or something new we want to try in the bedroom, or when one of us inadvertently steps on an emotional land mine. We never bottle anything up.

My future husband is my best friend. Just don't tell my sister that because she gets pissed whenever he says it.

"Shit, I forgot my wallet on the counter. I'll go grab it and be right back. There are at least two things in there I cannot wait for the honeymoon to use." Trent gives me one more kiss on the cheek, then turns back to jog the half block to the adult toy store we just spent several hours in.

I had wanted to shop for this stuff online, but Trent insisted going to a sex shop was a rite of passage, and I had to do it at least once. It turned out to be a ridiculous amount of fun. We laughed, made out a little, and made more purchases than I expected us to. It's a good thing we will be alone in the tropics for so long; we have a lot of product testing to do.

Which reminds me, I need to stock up on batteries before we leave.

"Francie?"

Dread billows up in my chest, freezing my lungs for a moment. I'd recognize that deep voice anywhere. It is the same voice that berated me and tore me down for years, until I was so filled with self-doubt I almost ruined the best thing to ever happen to me.

Turning, I look straight into the eyes of the man my younger, dumber self thought she loved. But now I see him for what he is: a weak man who took his insecurities out on his wife. The sad thing is, he isn't a bad looking guy. A little thick in the middle, but I never minded that. His hair is neat and trimmed with a little premature grey running through the brown, and his face is handsome with a strong chin. But his eyes are empty and his mouth stern.

"I'd heard rumors you'd turned into some sort of a sex addict, but really, this is just pathetic." Derek nods to the bags in my hands with the bright pink logo splashed across the sides. "You always were hard to please. Figures you would need all those contraptions to get a reaction."

The laugh bubbling up inside me cannot be contained, and I don't even try. "Derek, I am not hard to please, but it turns out I did need someone who gave even a little bit of a shit about me to be happy."

"I highly doubt any respectable man would allow you to bring all those . . . toys into the bedroom." Derek sneers as he says the word *toys*. As if they are filthy and below him.

Whatever. I really couldn't give two shits about what he thinks. But I do need to get him gone before Trent comes back with his wallet. If there is anything I know about my fiancé (eek! *fiancé*!), it is that he is extremely protective and possessive. We talked a lot about the scars my marriage left on me, and I know he wants nothing more than to make Derek eat his teeth.

"Well, it was completely unpleasant running into you, Derek. Bye. Hope to never see you again." I turn to walk back toward the store, needing to get away from my ex as soon as possible.

"Even back in high school, I knew there was nothing special about you. So frumpy and homely. I thought I could help mold you into an upstanding wife, but you resisted my suggestions at every turn." I can hear the disappointment in his voice, and a little teeny tiny part of me, buried way down deep under all the love Trent has shown me, hates knowing I've let Derek down. But I promptly kick that feeling to the curb and turn on my heel. Derek, oblivious as always, doesn't see the fire in my eyes and keeps droning on. "My mother warned me when we started dating that you would be no good. That you were too weak to handle a man of my stature. I should have listened."

Ugh. His mother. He is right; she always hated me. I was never near good enough for her little prince. I'm pretty sure she is half the reason he is the way he is. Being told over and over again your whole life that you can do no wrong and everyone else is to blame for everything bad that happens in your life is going to make a douche bag out of anyone. And I honestly believe that the other half of the blame lies on genetics, because everyone in his family seems to have the same affliction.

Behind me a low growl vibrates the air around us, the deep bass of that sound goes straight to my belly, curling my insides into a spiral of arousal.

"Who are you to talk to my wife that way?" Trent's long legs eat up the sidewalk that separates me from Derek, and if I'm not mistaken, I see genuine fear in my ex-husband's eyes. "No one talks to her with anything but respect and dignity. If they do, I end them."

I hold back the squeal that really, really wants to escape from my throat. I don't get to see the super jealous, possessive side of Trent often because there is never any reason for it to come out. Only an idiot would see us together and ever think it would be a good idea to approach me in any way, good or bad. But when it does come out, it makes me very happy, because I know I'll be in for a good, dirty, rough fucking when we get home. Trent will feel the need to stake his claim on me in the form of his handprint on my ass, his cum all over my chest and stomach, and my pussy sore from the pounding it will take. I almost rub my hands together in glee.

"W-w-wife. She's not your wife." Derek tries to take a few steps back, but Trent just follows. And then the douche canoe goes and makes everything worse. "She's my wife. Even though the courts dissolved our marriage, they can't do anything in the eyes of God."

I really can't help the way my eyes roll. Derek is religious only when it suits him, something I'm pretty sure God would take issue with.

"Wrong." Trent roars the word, and I get the craziest vision of him dressed up as the beast from *Beauty and the Beast*. Hmmm. Role-playing isn't something we've really explored yet. Note taken. "She is *my* wife."

"Technically, dear, I am your fiancé, but in a few weeks, yes, I will be your wife." I can't help but throw that in there, just for accuracy's sake.

Trent swings around to look at me, and his face softens slightly, because even worked up like this and ready to punch Derek in the face, Trent would never look at me with anything but love. God, he is the best.

"Semantics. You are my woman." Trent turns back to Derek, the hardness in his voice back in place. "She is my woman. You tried to cage her, tear her down and make her believe she couldn't do better. You were the one who couldn't do better. Now I get to reap what you threw away. You are an idiot. A small, weak idiot who likes to keep the women in your life under your heel. But she was too strong to allow you to do that. And now she is mine. I am hers. And if you don't get out of our general vicinity, I will end your worthless little life."

Apparently getting the picture, Derek turns without another word, and no joke, scampers away. Actually scampers. I can't help but giggle a little. How I ever thought I loved that man is beyond me. Now that I have Trent in my life, it seems impossible that anyone could have come before him.

Trent's shoulders rise up and slowly drop as he takes in a deep, steadying breath.

"I'm very proud of you for not hitting him." Wrapping my arms around Trent's waist, I bury my face into his strong back. Is it possible to smell testosterone? Because I swear the scent of power and man is wafting off him, soaking my lady bits.

"Gotta say, I'm proud of myself too." Trent turns and cradles my face between his large hands. All the anger and fire are gone from his eyes, replaced by concern and love.

"Are you okay? I only heard a little of what that asshat said to you, but none of it sounded pleasant."

"I'm fine. I was just about to give him what for when you showed up. Everything he said just blew right past me, for the most part." I turn my face to kiss each of his palms in succession. "He was right about one thing though. I'm never going to be an upstanding wife."

"Thank fuck for that. Even after we get married, you better stay my dirty as fuck wife. Screw upstanding. Now, let's go home. I'm putting that rabbit vibrator in your pussy, the plug in your ass, then I'm going to fuck your mouth. Just like I know you'll love."

"Fuck, I love you."

Trent flips me upside down over his shoulder, carrying me off in a fireman's carry. Then he slaps my ass for good measure.

"Love you too, my dirty fiancé."

EPILOGUE TWO
Two Years Later
Trent

"Do you think I should call and check on her?" Francie twists her fingers together in the seat next to me. The seat of our almost brand-new minivan.

Because I am minivan people now. Hell, yes, I am. We have one baby at home, our first, and I can't wait to fill up the rest of this van with more of them. The first moment our little girl, Celeste, blinked up at me with those grey-blue eyes all babies have, I was a goner. One hundred percent wrapped around her little finger. She isn't even a year, yet I am already looking at how much a pony costs.

But tonight isn't about our little angel. Tonight is about Francie and me reconnecting. Francie's sister, Meg, is spending the night at our house tonight so we can have our first night alone since the baby came. We need this time together. As much as I love our little Celeste, I feel as if we should have given her the middle name Cockblocker because that girl knows exactly when I am about to start in giving her mom what we both love so much. I can count on two hands the number of times we've been able to not only have sex, but finish sex, in the last ten months. And even those times were rushed.

I wouldn't change it though. Celeste is worth getting the occasional case of blue balls. And so will her siblings be once they come along.

"Honey, Celeste is going to be fine. You know how much she loves her Aunt Meg. They are going to have a great time tonight, and so are we. Then when we go back home tomorrow afternoon, we'll be even better parents for having given ourselves this time together." I reach over and grip Francie's hand, the one bearing my rings that I put on her finger two years ago this week.

"I know. I just miss her already. Is that crazy? I mean, we've only been gone for two hours. And dinner was amazing. But I just can't stop thinking about her." Francie falls silent for a moment before barreling on with all the little insecurities I know are rattling around in her head. "Do you think she is going to like Meg better than me? I know Meg really wants to be the cool aunt, so does that make me the uncool mom?"

"Don't you worry. Celeste will think you are the coolest. Until she reaches her teens and then every adult will be insufferably uncool." That at least gets a giggle out of my wife.

The ding of her phone fills the van, and Francie has the thing out of her purse and unlocked before I can even blink. "Oh, look how cute!" Francie turns the phone to me, and it is a selfie of Meg holding up the baby. They are both wearing matching Rainbow Brite pajamas.

"Where does she find these clothes? Rainbow Brite isn't even a thing anymore, is it?" I don't know which one of them spends more money on that baby, Francie or her sister. It is a good thing Meg found an equally rich husband to settle down with.

Another ding comes through, and Francie reads the text out loud to me. "I can feel you worrying from here. We are fine. Have fun."

"See, everything is good. Let's just concentrate on us tonight."

Francie nods in her seat beside me, letting out the pent-up breath I know she's been holding since we left the house. "Speaking of which, where the hell are you taking me right now? I don't recognize anything."

"Ah-ha, finally clued in to that, did you? It is a surprise. That is all you are getting out of me." I love surprising my dirty girl. The expression she gets when it all comes together is one of my favorite things on this earth.

Right as the words leave my lips, we pull into the parking lot of what looks like a completely unassuming country club. The grounds are manicured to perfection, and the sprawling building has spotlights featuring different architectural details. As I pull up to the valet station, I sneak a peek over at my wife. Her jaw is on the floor, and her eyes are as big as I've ever seen them.

"Oh my gosh, this place is amazing!" The awe in her voice is unmistakable.

"You haven't seen the half of it, honey." I exit the van, going to the back to grab our overnight bag, which Meg packed earlier in the day. By the time I make it to the passenger side of the van, Francie is already standing there looking around at the lush gardens, visible thanks to the full moon shining overhead.

"Is this where we are staying tonight?" She laces her fingers with mine and wraps her other arm around my bicep, leaning her head against my shoulder.

"Yes. Among other things."

Tilting her face up to mine, Francie gives me a quizzical look. But I simply kiss her nose and lead her into the club.

It may look like a country club, but no one would guess it is actually a highly selective sex club. We won't be participating in any of the festivities that take place on the lower levels of Club Zion, but we will be observing. Francie has always wanted to watch a couple have sex in real life, not just the porn we occasionally watch together. She has a little bit of a voyeur in her and a little bit of an exhibitionist. We're very fond of finding dark corners to christen, never someplace that could get us in serious trouble and never someplace where there is a real danger of us being seen. She likes the thrill of the possibility. Not the actual act of having sex in front of others. But she loves watching. Mirrors are a big thing with us.

There is no need to check in since I've already taken care of all of those arrangements. Instead, we are escorted straight to the suite I've reserved for the night. We have about an hour to kill before the festivities downstairs will begin.

When we met three years ago, I thought it was impossible to love her any more than I did. Then it just grew and grew every day. On our wedding day, I thought that had to be it, our love had grown as much as it could, and we would forever be in that state of love and bliss. Then she gave me a daughter, and watching her with our child has made my love grow exponentially. I've finally accepted that our love will never stop expanding.

As I lead her to the bathroom, where I have a bubble bath, champagne, and candles waiting for her, that love consumes me to the point of near pain. I leave her alone to relax in silence, something she rarely gets these days. A half an hour later she steps from the bathroom, glowing and fresh, and it takes everything I have not to take her to the ground and fuck her into tomorrow. But I want to see her face when she realizes what this place is.

The outfit I picked out for her, with the help of her sister of course, is laying on the bed. It's a tight red skirt, almost modest in cut. The hem goes down to just above her knees. The shirt is a crop top that leaves just an inch or two of her sexy-as-hell tummy visible above the high waist of her skirt, and the neckline somehow manages to cover her more than ample chest.

Once I have us dressed and ready to go, we make our way to the elevator, Francie shooting me curious glances the whole time. "So, are we going dancing or something? What else could we be doing this late at night dressed up like this?"

Giving her the smile that she calls my up-to-no-good smile, I wrap my arm around her waist and draw her in tight to my side. "You'll just have to wait and see."

The elevator descends past the lobby, then stops at the first sublevel. Before it opens, a slot under the buttons for each floor lights up. I insert my key card for the room, and we are granted access into Club Zion.

It is apparent the moment we step off the elevator that this is no regular club. Men and women dressed in little to nothing walk around carrying trays of cocktails, serving them to yet more men and women in all states of dress. Some are wearing clothes similar to Francie and me, dresses and slacks and dress shirts. Some wear leather. Some wear nothing at all.

I turn to Francie as she takes it all in, her eyes round and curious. Her eyes follow a woman who has a foxtail dangling from her ass, undoubtedly attached to an anal plug, and nothing else on her body.

"Trent, where are we?" Her voice shakes a little, but not with fear. I know every sound this woman makes, and this one is all excitement.

"Welcome to Club Zion, the world's most exclusive sex club. Every kink you could possibly be curious about is represented here, all on display for your viewing pleasure. We can finally cross off the 'watch another couple have sex' item off your list." Taking her hand in mine, we wander into the lobby. All around us, people are talking, kissing, fucking. There are rooms lining the perimeter of the lobby, each with a sign explaining the theme of that room for the night.

According to Razor, who vouched for me to the club's owner, the themes change nightly, but scenes, as he calls them, break out spontaneously throughout the place as well.

"From the looks of it, we can cross this item off the list so many times we'll tear through the paper." Francie smiles up at me with that Cheshire grin, the one that lets me know she's making plans for us for later.

And yes, we still have the list. Francie framed it, actually. There are still three things left unchecked on the list: watch other people have sex in person, be watched while having sex, and sex with two men. This is the last item on the list that will ever be crossed off.

For a little while we wander from room to room, Francie's eyes taking everything in and her cheeks flaming bright red. Some rooms we don't linger in for all that long, mostly the ones involving BDSM or anything pain-related. Others, Francie is especially drawn to. The one where a woman is tied to the wall as people bring her nearer and nearer to orgasm seems to especially fascinate her. The sign outside the door said it was the forced edging room, and a list of rules stated that she could be brought to the brink of orgasm by any means necessary except actual penetrative sex.

After twenty minutes of watching the woman writhe and moan, we move on to another room. For the most part, we keep quiet, letting small touches and glances do the communicating for us.

But then we come to the free-for-all room. All around, people are screwing in all different configurations. We stand along the wall once again, just watching. Francie's breathing picks up pace, and I know she loves what she is seeing. She's confided to me in the past that when she meets someone, the first thing she wonders is how they like to have sex. It is one of many little quirks that I love. She is a sexual being through and through, and all mine. Here she can satisfy her kinky curiosities to no end.

I position her in front of me, not in an effort to hide my erection, because that would be pointless in a place like this. No, I move her there so I can whisper in her ear and have access to her body.

Indicating a pairing of two men and one woman across the room, I lean down to ask the question I've never broached with her since the night with Razor. "Do you ever wish we had gone through with it?"

"Never." She leans her head back on my shoulder so she can look me in the eye. "You fill me up more than multiple partners ever could. Not just sexually, though you are very good at that, too." She gives me her wicked grin again. "But in my soul. In my heart. You fill every inch of my life with love and trust. I could never regret not doing something that could have caused damage to that. I'm not even curious about it anymore. Everything we've done in bed has more than satisfied my curiosity on that particular item."

I always knew that was how she felt, but it is still nice hearing it confirmed again. "But you like your surprise, right?"

Looking out over the room again, Francie takes it all in. "I won't lie. This is all very hot. I would never want to join in, but watching people in this state, in the throes of passion, I can't deny it fascinates me." She rubs her ample ass against the bulge in my pants and laughs a little. "Obviously, you like it as well."

I can't help but laugh and groan at the same time as she does a little wiggle against my cock. "Sure, it would be near impossible to walk into a place like this and not immediately pop some wood. But honestly, this is how I am whenever I have you in my arms. You know that."

"I do." I can hear the smile in her voice.

"I'm also thinking about all the things I'm going to do with this body tonight." Snaking one of my arms around her body, I press my fingers down into the waist of her skirt, rubbing over the silk panties I insisted she wear. No way was I letting her come to a sex club with no panties on. "First, I'm going to eat your succulent pussy until I'm completely satisfied. It won't be for your pleasure, though you can be sure you will get plenty. It will be all for me, because there is nothing I love more than tasting your cream." I dip my fingers under the soaked fabric, sliding them along her slit, but not touching her clit just yet. "Then I'm going to put you to your knees, just like that guy over there." I indicate the man a few feet from us going to town on another man's cock. "And you'll suck me down into your throat until you almost can't breathe."

Francie writhes against me but doesn't let a sound out, not even a whimper. She knows no one is allowed to hear her needy little noises but me.

"Then I'll lay you down on the bed and tease your entrance with the tip of my cock until you beg me for more." I mimic what I've just described with the tip of my finger.

"Trent, please, what will you do to me then?" Francie's voice is breathless, and I can sense the struggle in her body not to get too worked up.

"Then I'm going to push my cock deep inside you and give you the dirtiest fucking missionary sex of your life." Francie laughs out loud, several people nearby pausing their various ministrations to look in our direction. She turns in my arms, removing my hand from her skirt, and laughs uncontrollably against my shirt.

Once she has her little burst under control, Francie looks up at me with shining eyes. "Take me upstairs, and give it to me old faithful-style. Now, please."

I lean down, giving her a brief but passionate kiss. "Whatever you say, dear. And if you're good, tomorrow morning I'll let you sleep until noon so you'll still get a full eight hours of sleep despite my fucking you all night."

"Oh God, you really know how to speak my language, dirty husband." The world around us fades away. For a moment, it is just Francie and me gazing into each other's eyes like the lovesick fools we are, and always will be. "I love you."

"I love you too, my dirty wife."

ABOUT THE AUTHOR

Brandy Ayers is a writer of erotic romance. Or romantic erotica, depending on how you look at it. She has been telling stories in one form or another since she was a child and decided her English / Irish heritage was boring. Instead, for a 4th grade class genealogy assignment, she weaved a tale of mystery and intrigue about her great, great grandpa chief of the Navajo tribe. No one bought it. Brandy lives in Pennsylvania with her husband, son, daughter, neurotic boxer, and Satan worshipping cat.

Made in the USA
Las Vegas, NV
30 April 2025